# BRADFORD LIBRARIES

B19

CU00912017

Also by Gee Williams

*Magic and Other Deceptions*
*Salvage*
*Blood, etc*

# A GIRL'S ARM
# GEE WILLIAMS

SALT

LONDON

PUBLISHED BY SALT PUBLISHING

Acre House, 11 – 15 William Road, London NW1 3ER United Kingdom

© Gee Williams, 2012

First published by Salt Publishing, 2012

Printed in Great Britain by the MPG Books Group, Bodmin and King's Lynn

Typeset in Paperback 9.5 / 14.5

ISBN 978 1 97773 19 8 paperback

*To David*
*and for Kate and Simon Long*

# CONTENTS

The Knight's Move     1

The Chameleon     18

Barley Rogers     27

False Banded     50

Eyeful     69

A Crack     81

That Story     101

Settled at Civeen     120

Roof     142

A Christmas Birthday     151

A Girl's Arm     169

*Acknowledgments*     227

# A GIRL'S ARM

# THE KNIGHT'S MOVE

*I did a dreadful thing ...*

The torn slip of paper she'd written on refused to settle. If she'd managed to keep it flat, that would have helped. But to crumple and then try to restore by stroking gave the page an extra dynamic. She turned away too quickly and the air found out the creases, had it in motion, describing an arc that took it behind her back and under a seat. The second time it fluttered to her feet.

A last look around the room: the blinds were half drawn against the street and their strings fastened in the metal keepers. Illumination enough for someone – Ian – coming in before dark, as was possible. The sofa, caught with her knee in pursuit of the note, needed straightening so that nothing stood out as different or was going to be indicative. A CD had been left propped against the wooden box where they kept pens and receipts and oddments. She replaced John Russell's *Hyste* into the rack. Hating it – hating most of Ian's music – the black cross of its cover blurred as though precious to her.

A good way to do it. She had been antsy to get going from the thought's first arrival on waking. A great way. The ease of the drive up appeared to validate the decision in every clear lane of motorway and every green light once off it. South Lancashire to the Northern Lakes – a journey lengthy in memory with complaints from all but Piet Keller and impeded when the club Landrover actually cut out – she did this time in an hour and a half. Onto minor roads, her gear rattled in the back seat . . . they had been a superstitious crew, Jo especially. Equipment for instance: the wire slings must be laid out with chocks pointing downward, red ropes were used for climbing, never for abseils. *Exactly ninety minutes* – she could hear Jo's voice, the soft Lallans of it – *now that's a real sign.*

It was a fine October morning. Dry and that north-westerly off Derwent Water would cool the hands; but the bag of chalk she'd hung at her waist meant she'd still be leaving white streaks, arrows to her ascent. From the empty lay-by where she only just thought to lock her car, she fought through blackthorn and nettle to the base of an escarpment of hard grey Rhyolite, greened at its feet and rising in her imagination to a coarse crown, ninety metres above. She had missed her path – otherwise Falcon Crag seemed completely unchanged, which was just as well, being the reason she was here.

It had been nearly twenty years. Once before on this spot there had been a period of discussion she was involved in. Who would go with whom, who would take which route, who would lead? Ian, Mick and Jo had made up a three and left them. They clanked off, out of sight, towards the Hedera

Grooves ascent they would never finish. Nothing else was said, once decided – what was there? She got Piet, had got the Lamplighter route, had got to lead because Piet was less experienced than herself. He was a head taller, half as strong again and looked as if he could do anything. Yet, 'Makes sense,' he agreed. A face tanned since birth by the African sun never showed much.

Today she had no need for negotiation. To the solitary raven wheeling in the direction of Low Moss she said, 'I get to lead. I take Lamplighter,' because she intended to do it solo and free – to almost do it. She unshouldered the small rucksack and changed into the pair of sticky-soled Boreals she'd always worn. They were much older than the boots she took off. What to do with the boots? Lobbing them separately into the undergrowth was a possibility but felt wrong. The laces pulled through and neat, she settled for leaving them side by side about a metre up, neither hidden nor obvious. Such was the strength of recalled experience that the weathered hands doing the tidying seemed unfamiliar – as were the rings and the nails on which varnish was beginning to retreat from the tips. She had been unencumbered then . . . She pushed the boots as far back as they would go. Their owner might return, they said. A miniature birch corkscrewing out of a cleft could be their marker.

*We split into separate parties. Piet and I roped up. We had two ropes, red for going up – a longer black for down that went in Piet's pack. We put on harnesses, bought for the trip in his case, better than mine. We got ready pretty briskly. I ran through the details again for Piet. The first pitch – not too bad, the second much harder with a crux, the Knight's Move,*

*named as the bit most likely to deck you. I took wire slings
with carabiners already on – mated we call it – two homemade nylon straps and the rope tied to a big screw-gate at my
back and we were ready. I'd done similar but not here and not
with Piet. I was slightly nervous but not frightened. I wanted
to go. I started. The first few metres were easy and the rock
seemed good and hard, sharp in places – and no vegetation.
It's climbed often and the locals clean it once a season. No – no
problem with grip not with these shoes and my fingers felt like
suckers. I stood out from the surface as it went away from me
maybe thirty degrees, moving quickly and building a rhythm
so as not to rest too long. You need to step from one small ledge
or balance to another and work from hold to hold as fast as
your eye picks them out.*

Why wait this time? She took it quickly, sensing behind
her the reassurance of timber, oak and ash with their open
arms and cushioning foliage. To feel so confident was unex-
pected, but then the first pitch was still easy enabling her to
look around, the illusion being the climb was through the
trees, that she was an animal of the forest. Beyond thirty-
five metres came a wide stance listed as the first belay
point. She tied on where the book said, around a flake at
the back of the stance. Then, as now, it had been enjoyable
and thoughtfree, though she said neither when questioned.
Nor that she'd felt weightless.

But so far so flattering – the years had taken nothing, her
arms promised and the calf muscles crowed. Then *Sober
up!* she told herself. To go off from here would be . . . unfit-
ting. Lamplighter was climbable by a good leader and a less
good second if you didn't alternate and with Piet it hadn't

4

been her intention. It was defined as VS. The modern mania for subtler grades in alphanumeric had taken over since, but she remained satisfied with Very Severe: exposure and testing moves.

*As I said, no problem and when I yelled ready, Piet yelled climbing and he followed me up. He took it slow – looked calm. You don't want to see your second come in a rush just because you're watching them. This was about right.*

It was a lie. Piet had barged up to the first stance, the bright blob of his helmet always mobile as he searched for leverage, his muscles – that trapezius power – getting him out of trouble more than once and losing tension in the rope. Nobody appreciated that. 'You're a bit premature,' she said. If he heard, if he comprehended, he didn't respond.

*We stood and edged around each other till he tied on as well. I left him to haul up the pack.*

But she had the stance to herself – of course she did. Round about now, Ian would be punishing his calluses under the desk, dreaming of escape from the departmental meeting. Mick and Jo were doing something the same elsewhere, probably. She had an idea about the lives they'd settled for and it would be a case of settling, once you'd done this. Jo's children maybe made it easier . . .

. . . So alone and climbing free. 'Bouldering' it had been called in the days of the university club because nobody was doing much free work back then. Free meant an absence of ropes – like *this,* taking the holds where they invited, up and to the right, a sixty degree sidle towards the first pause. It meant having no second with their slight tension always on you, utile as an extra limb. Free, as in free to go off the next instant – or this one now because it has arrived.

She forced a halt. She might pay for it later when being below par would tell, but it was important to visualise the ascent again. Annoyingly there were paintmarkers in places that led entirely in the wrong direction where technical climbers had been out setting up routes for themselves. Just as they had scorned the boulderers, so they had mocked the 'screw-fix' merchants' hammers and drills, defeating the rock with a permanent ladder of ironmongery. They had been the true-shillings they believed, in whatever combination they cared to present to the task: Ian and herself, Mick, two of Mick's mates, both names long-eroded, and Jo – and Piet joining last of all. That got her moving. Above the treeline the huge expanse of the lake came into sight, its radiance almost palpable over either shoulder. Extreme beauty was what she recalled here, as the great gap in the Cumbrian Mountains that began all the way down in Borrowdale, opened to her elevation. But the failure of branches brought exposure and a noticeable blow. Pitch 2 was indeed Very Severe, the holds fewer and smaller. Then halfway up it turned interesting. A hold she had tested with arm-weight failed as soon as she loaded it with even a tad extra. Her fingers jerked out from the indent, leaving her hopes on one good left hand lock and the shallow niche for a set of toes in the point of the right shoe –

Wouldn't do! Panic bursting out of her, she kissed the rock, laying as much cloth and skin as she had against it while flattening the traitorous hand on a boss that felt polished, that was nothing at all really, that was gone anyway and . . . But friction rewarded her with stillness though it was a fragile state a trickle of sweat could undo. A breath was a gamble. Before she could debate with herself the meaning of this fear she found a better hold – it had been there all along – and pushed on, taking a mental tongue-lashing. Concentration must be intense however seductive the scenery: if the first pitch was sweet and arboreal, the second was coming as a shock in its malevolence.

Her name was Lorna, surname Wintersgill, Ian's name. She was celebrating her birthday on this fourth day of the tenth month. A sign. She had left home after breakfast – an ordinary breakfast, starving was an idiot's preparation – without, in the end, leaving a note. She had driven up to Derwent Water, the gem in Lakeland's hoard and, at eleven o'clock on a Monday morning, she was embracing a slab of solidified lava that had once been extruded by unimaginable force then thrust aside by glaciation. A metre off the ground for every year of her age, she was a forty year old woman who hadn't climbed for several seasons so amazement was giving way to guilty pleasure at even this minimal achievement – so far. In the pocket of the zippity covering her upper body was a slip of paper with its scrawled opening line. *I did a dreadful thing . . .*

Soon – because Ian had been a good partner and deserved better than burdening – she would get the note out and get rid. When she had a moment to spare. When she had more than two points of contact which wasn't now. Time to make progress.

After a short but absorbing section where the rock wasn't sound, it became almost straightforward; her route traced a ridge with grips either side, finger pressure being enough for steadiness. If not feeling exactly weightless this time round, she could do no wrong. Each hand and foot was rewarded with purchase at the first ask and she longed for Ian there to witness it even as the thought was counter-punched: if you were going so well, how explain the result?

*So far I'd put in no protection so Piet hadn't had to take any out on his way up. That wouldn't last. He arrived and we shared a belay for about ten seconds before I got another chock in a crack and tied on that.*

The last trees were far below but the rumble of invis-ible traffic on the road drifted up – many more vehicles now than there were then; in intervals came the spoken exchanges of tourists on the lake edge. Colder air meant the rock felt moist to the touch and she chalked oftener as the plane she tried to adhere to came ever closer to the vertical. Through a column of nothingness, she clawed her way.

*I thought I would start putting in a few nuts as I went, for Piet.*

No point in that now – the holds were small but still sur-prisingly good, if you had fingertip strength and the ankles held out. The inclination was still to the right rather than straight up.

*I slipped the first nut in – then the rope through the cara-biner. The idea is if you go off your second has got you on that nut – but it's as far again below before you stop. You better keep it tighter, I shouted. There's one in here, see it? Piet said yes and*

*I could picture him leaning out to look with the red rope around his back and crossed over his body to take the weight if I fell . . .*

Another three metres and here was what it was all about, the Knight's Move.

The book said holds ran out on this section for the 'natural' way up. Either you must go artificial and put in bolts – or proceed one step right and two steps up, becoming the knight on a giant's upended chessboard. And the step-ups were over the far side of a ridge. Think the crest on a newt's back but carved in stone, a perverse bit of geology blocking the ascent. Your line of sight must be craned for around it. That tentative first foot had to go up and over, groping its way so that the next could cross the crest in turn. But not to join – the two footholds were directly above each other. Right then left, both to be placed at predetermined points on the $y$ axis of the graph. As Ian had said *otherwise what was hard enough to make it a named move?* The hands weren't so badly off. There were small but reasonable holds though these were chest-low: the closer to the heart the hold, the more the pulse upped itself, as a climber's shifting centre of gravity offered to make a pinwheel of the limbs.

And to survive you needed to get to the next novelty, a hand-jam. It was the first one on the entire climb, a hand-jam in a crack that also ran up the face, well above head height. So it was 'two moves . . . then wedge your hand in fairly quickly to make the next. Don't consider it!' But Ian held her eyes longer than was needed, willing her agreement. 'Don't think, you daft cow – do it.'

He'd think though, when she didn't return, of that other

day. Every word and everything not said was drilled and fixed into each of them by Piet's fall, half a life ago. Ian would know exactly where the mistake was made – Ian with his long stare, his loving *daft cow!* For a flash she almost changed her mind. That arc of sky, the only thing she dared look at, had the sheen of a dove's breast – white, silver, lemon, forget-me-not. Incredible. And a woman's squeal of laughter and the deeper response told her someone had entered the trees from the lay-by, were maybe considering Lamplighter and the Knight's Move, as she had completed it once, Piet below to take her if she went, of course, but still . . . routes such as this one were the point of existence, were about the living thing's enduring through moment after moment, its faith in the unbroken chain.

But she was here now.

An inelegant shuffle sideways until the crest is next to her and she is standing on a good shelf with weight distrib-uted, fingers resting lightly in their shallow holds. Now she moves the right foot and lifts it over the crest to the nubbin of rock, raises her body using every flexion point, putting some strain on the knee but a single leg lift isn't so bad even this one . . . She weighs what she did at twenty, after all. The left hand is offering some though not much aid because it's lined up with her belly-button and at the level of her sternum. Pulling down is torture. Pushing up, though – in a second she can raise herself to turn the hand, press the rock with the flat of it – will be ecstasy in comparison. And the hold is keeping her upright, taking almost no weight at all. Even so, a tremor stirs in her triceps. A ticking clock. The left foot starts over the crest and now her right hand goes up like a child's in her class. It fumbles the crack, folds its own thumb in then widens again to fill the space. Her left foot is joining them now; it probes for the high step, it's baffled, *it finds it* and her complete frame is over. Once again her weight is above her feet, giving an instant of stability on the toes. She is held in place but without any lateral equilibrium. This way or that? In which direction will she topple? Now another single-leg body lift, this time with the left, not so strong. But it's nothing, a staircase tread and her grip is high and can help. The right foot slides across . . . up to the wonderful, wonderful ledge, a ledge that will accept a Boreal's toe *and* heel and does . . . then that hand is freed from the vice of the jam to a wide hold, the other relaxes and rises to meet it. And she is steady at last on a stance that to senses freshly schooled by the rock is generous enough for sleep.

She let her head droop forward until there was the tap of protective shell against Falcon Crag. Her attention strayed inward, riding the channels and surges within her entire self, the taut fibres' slow release, the cartilages' shrugging off of compression. Adrenalin was breaking down. The tingling in her chest cavity that she hadn't even registered stopped abruptly. Muscles dekinked. No more John Russell rhythms. Everything quietened. Even the voices that had hurried her forward in those last few seconds had faded out, surrendering her sole possession of Lamplighter.

But all the motorway miles of the journey it had never

occurred that she would not have it to herself, nor that she would be standing here.

The next few metres were climbing-wall easy as they began sloping away from the huge pull of Derwent's valley. Hips and belly and breasts brushed smooth hardness and her centre, deep in the pelvis, felt her weight working through the solid mass of the crag instead of vacancy. Then she was at the top. She fastened on to a steel stake pounded in by the local club for that purpose before flipping onto her back and elbows, gulping air. The west was tending to proper blue and the lake seemed almost touchable. Out there she counted off islands that she could put a name to, St Herbert's and Lords for certain and –

All just as she had done on that day, waiting.

*Secure, I called down to Piet.*

It should have allowed him to relax and not think *disaster!* at the rope's twitch. As for her, no time for gloating – she must award herself retrospective points, she realised. Leather fingerless gloves had come straight out. She tugged them on before winding in the slack, slipping it around her shoulders. She moved to the end of the tie-on, braced against an outcrop with her left foot and, feeling tension in the back runner that held her in place, called out.

*Ready? I concentrated on fetching him up. I took in rope as he came through the first easy moves – then I must have been anticipating. The rope went too tight. I eased off – presumed he was paused, thinking. The leader mustn't encourage the second with the rope. I leaned against the tie-on to look over the edge. Saw him. Vapour-locked.*

Did they say that back in nineteen-ninety? Frozen, then.

The legs and the arms with the bunched biceps were set solid. But on the rock there could be no rest, even tied on; there was respite but not rest. And after all that rushing, it seemed Piet was stalled.

'Piet?' she had called.

Nothing happened.

'Piet?' On the far side of the newt's crest his feet were together – too close together she thought – but positioned to make the Knight's Move. She let her eyes dart out to the marvel of water. He would speak first – she could rely on that, even from Piet whom she relied on least, though technically he could outdo Mick now. Among themselves they'd agreed that Piet would turn out to be 'pretty sound.' He didn't bother to call them by name. His rare jokes were turned never against himself, always against Jo or her. Neither could stand him, not that they felt the need to share. What did it matter on the rock? She returned her attention to where it ought to be. Nothing had changed. Planted there, the stupid, brash orange of his helmet glowed against the drabness.

*I don't know how long. A while.*

More in boredom than in anger, that's how she remembered it done. If he'd acknowledged her, made a sound, she would never have teased the pebble over – not even a pebble, a shard more like. More threatening debris had fallen during the climb, had caught her. That's what headgear was for, keeping you safe from above. And the one thing everyone knew about Falcon Crag was that the rock *could* be rotten . . . 'wersh', as Jo said, her general term for feeble.

She had chosen her missile, watched its launch and trajectory. Next would come the ping on his helmet and a reaction. But then Piet looked up – finally, with those fish eyes of his and the dark speck that she'd already lost sight of fell into the blue round of his iris . . . and that was it. Just that. A low, barely vocalised *ump* and he was off. He seemed to lurch onto the void: grabbing at the cliff face, he screamed as his fingertips were scoured away. She wrenched the rope across her body, felt the friction like a brand on her back, and the snatch and burn across both palms even through gloves. Piet started to spin as the rope tightened. He hit the rock once, twice with his head and the orange helmet bloomed with a lightning flash of bare metal. Then, mercifully the dragging on her stopped as the rope ended its slide through. But Kernmantle rope stretches maybe ten percent. He kept going down, the mist of blood surrounding his face blowing away as he dropped. He hit a third time. Here the blood showed as a vivid stream splattering the grey, gobbets of it thrown free through the air before the crag dealt him the final blow. He came to rest, his harnessed body horizontal. A thick gout of blood was expelled with the breath and then he failed with the next one, a sort of convulsion taking him in lieu. After that only a gentle rotation remained of all his stored energy, Piet a compass needle, west, south by south west, due south to Borrowdale . . . and there wasn't an instant of the occurrence when she didn't understand what had caused it, what happened and what to do. She called his name without response but she knew Piet was safe from the drop and from added strikes now. He was drowning, though. If she started to lower him she'd finish with a Piet even further from her and any assistance. There wasn't a choice. He had maybe twenty metres at most to ground and she slacked off and let him run out slowly. But he weighed so much more and the earth snatched him to it, searing her palms. *Stop him*! She tried and in wrenching the rope again smelled the burnt fabric of her clothing.

Every time, forever after, when a hot iron was put down . . .

He stopped. He had maybe ten metres to travel was her estimate. *Now again*. A fractional release and away he went, the rope burring before she braked him this time so acceleration shouldn't win. Her hands were on fire. Another stop . . . at three metres now or that was her instinct. One more: the heat took on a new intensity as the gloves burnt through. She crossed her wrists just as Piet reached the ground, signalled by the rope's sudden limpness and the easing of pain.

It took effort to unclench, another to take a full inhalation. When she hung over the edge there was the familiar jagged profile below with a bloody tagging of Piet's impacts – and then the quiescent crowns of oak.

The black rope was lost with Piet but there should be just enough red for her to reach the ground, anchored below by a dying or dead man. Yet she hesitated, staring in every direction. Out on Derwent Water a dinghy's white sail caught the breeze and from a lazy roll, it skittered over the surface . . . she considered a hike down from the top, round the back, safe and certain. No-one else was in sight but she shouted. It seemed necessary. For answer, a long way off somebody began ringing in a piton with a hammer, Ian perhaps. It's his unruffled tone that she adopts, asking herself: How many minutes have you used already?

Abseiling is a controlled fall. Thanks to Piet there was too little play but the figure-of-eight descender would let her throttle back the rate at which she joined him. She withdrew to the lip and slowly toppled over. *It's as fast as I dare, Ian.* One bounce must take her close to the Knight's Move but she wasn't noticing. A few metres above the body, she brought herself to a painful stop then became a spider and walked down the wall to him. She unclipped and was free.

She had heard it said, 'he could have been asleep.' Piet could not have been asleep in the weird tumble of parts and gear his physique had got itself into, his face hidden from her by brush, one arm seeming to reach inside his own vest. The other topped with a ruined hand clutched the skirt of the cliff as though ready to heave him upright. Quite calmly, knowing he had died, she took the orange helmet between her palms and turned it. The brows and one cheekbone were a single swipe of flayed skin and tissue like prime steak. Somewhere in there both eyes were open but with the pupils rolled up and lost, the whites livid. Piet's nose was the worst feature, a mashed ruddy fruit she feared to touch even with a hand's shadow. Fresh blood was still flowing from a grotesque pit, once discrete nostrils. But ajar and almost undamaged, the lips were Piet's, recognisably. She pushed two fingers in and back over his palate and felt the hot, live tongue.

He coughed blood and saliva and something else, not

quite liquid, straight into her mouth. She spat out *sorry!* as more dripped across her vision . . .

. . . which, today, is superhuman in clarity and can distinguish individual trees on Catbells, the sprawling hill that forms the western shore of the lake. She identifies bare Grassmoor and Grizedale Pike beyond and the glint of Bassenthwaite to the north. In her judgement the modest Derwent has carved out a masterpiece; nowhere is more impeccable. The fact that she had not expected to see this again can neither improve upon nor taint its perfection. You give a river fifteen million years, boil, freeze, choke and release and here's what it can do. Despite the endurance of rock, water trumps it.

She is God looking upon Her works.

Directly below, the voices of Man and Woman are calling again, moving away to her left though – definitely not attempting the Knight's Move. Her pronouncement? Wise.

And somewhere, Piet is. She needs to remind herself often. Also that she saved his life though too slowly. In the years following, through her ruthless twenties when a lot was going on, easy to agree with Ian, Jo and the others *better to have died . . . if it was me I wouldn't want to be left like that, you know . . . not if it was me.* The next decade has been less assured.

Her face flames at the thought that she has an opinion, she of all people.

# THE CHAMELEON

*Mortlake. A neo-Tudor house of three storeys and eccentric
detailing, a couple of miles south west of Chester on the Welsh
side of the River Dee. Its façade is particularly impressive with
extensive decorative timber work between sandstone chimney
stacks. The east wing is fronted by a huge jettied gable. Pevsner
called it a 'masquerade in oak and tile'....*

A.V. DODD (1982) *Welsh Border Houses*

Twice, soon to be three times, Fay Blethyn has used it as a
setting for her fiction. The research has all been done, you
could say. Firstly it was home to a decent enough couple
with crippling debts and a twisted little scheme for getting
out again. More recently, in an act of malice, she made it
headquarters to a repellent cult. A modern Svengali takes
over and one of her characters becomes involved with him
– violently. Some trait of the building acting as a catalyst . . .
is one interpretation. In the last chapter it burns.

But Mortlake is still there. The pocket-park which
seemed endlessly expansive has been eaten away and built
up along the margins. A new by-pass took another slice.
Some of its interior treasures may have been ripped out
by this time, exported even. But the house stands, though

subdivided and more ordinary with its spell broken. Or so she believes.

As a child in the late nineteen-sixties, she and her mother came there on a brilliant blue morning. The mother, pedalling for half an hour along Flintshire's border, had seven-year-old Fay perched behind on a seat. Although much nearer town than their own village, the area they were coming to was wooded and seemingly more natural – more 'countrified'. In reality, Edwardian planting had matured; fir and rampant laurel meant the house was barely visible through olive shade. As they crunched up the drive, the mother now wheeling, it had to be taken on trust that Mortlake existed at all. But it did and her mother had come to clean it.

By a circular route past empty coach house and stables, they were entering an Arts and Crafts Gentleman's Residence. Basically a country house and estate had been scaled down to early twentieth century taste. Apart from a sprawling, half-timbered manor built in 1919 but with all the feudal necessities of staff quarters and back stairs, as well as grand rooms just for show, there were acres of grounds. These had been laid out by Clough Williams Ellis, it was claimed – not that it would have meant anything to either of them at the time – and came complete with the full Arcadian set: a small lake, thatched gazebo, formal lawns, a serpentine walk ending in a glimpse of the Welsh hills and a 'wilderness' of flowering trees and shrubs. Not quite fitting into all this was the turquoise swimming pool that could be filled from the lake and emptied back into it through a secret system of pipes and pumps, now defunct. Every cliché was assembled for melodrama.

The mother had been taken on for five mornings a week, nine till twelve. Most of her work was of the dust-harassing variety. Bright Persian rugs and runners and the polished parquet they rested on, all had to be attacked with a monster Hoover that had more appendages than the Hydra. The freshening up of empty guest suites, each bathroom fitted into a panelled compartment airless as a priest's hole, was another daily duty. An unused nugget of lavender soap must be turned over. A dry basin must be rinsed. The huge house completely swamped just three occupants: the Sobels, an elderly English couple, and their housekeeper, a spinster (her mother always used the term, spitting it out like an expletive), Hatty Harris. She was a heavy woman, swollen jointed by arthritis but with a round unlined face. She dressed in not-quite a uniform: dark skirts and cardigans always and blue blouses that bulged with a glimpse of the harnessed mottled flesh between button holes, ugly and compelling at the same time. From the Sobels' treatment of her and the vantage point of adulthood, Fay understood she must have been with them for decades, not quite a servant. Hatty – who didn't even 'talk nice' her mother noted, who was 'no better than us' – had her own sitting room next to the kitchen. Here were displayed treasures untouchable by the cleaner's child, mostly knick-knacks from the Sobels' daughter and grandchildren, all living abroad now.

And here was one cause of the trouble.

From the first morning of Fay's appearance at Mortlake,

the Sobels were taken with the novelty of a child's coming
into their closed world. Her mother had been hired by
Hatty on the understanding that Fay would be invisible.
She would play out of doors weather permitting; the walled
Herbery was meant to be secure. When not, she was to be
fixed at her mother's side as though by elastic. Getting her
out was no problem. The park was easily accessed and a
paradise – and is still in Fay's memory, though she has
seen its mutilation. Her own imaginings were more than
sufficient company and there was plenty for them to work
on, like the pewter lake with its bushy island and spongy-
bottomed rowing boat. Better still, the lurid swimming
pool held a few inches of rainwater at one end and a ladder
finishing half way down in nothingness. The ornamental
structures of a designed landscape were all to be pried into
. . . and there was more wildlife than you ever got on the
scabby pastures around home. Her first red squirrel not
in a book was so exquisite it almost stopped her breath.
Caught feeding on one of the fir cones that fell everywhere,
it bolted only when she could stay frozen not a moment
longer . . . whereas the lake's giant fish retained patches of
gilding that let her recognise individuals and follow their
progress from the bank for as long as interest lasted. Was
her mother lax – or just too desperate for the job? Both. In
hospital Fay's father lay stricken and facing years of inva-
lidity. Fay had been the last, inconvenient child of middle
age. That she could amuse herself, or be enticed into the
library where Mrs Sobel reclined on the world's longest
sofa, must have seemed a godsend.

*The Library: in contrast to the drawing room, the library is a masculine though not austere space, lesser in size. Bookcases by Gillows are of mahogany with glazed and gilt doors. But an inset limewood carving used as part of the chimneypiece is probably the finest acquisition in the entire house. Measuring only twenty-nine inches by eighteen it depicts an owl perched upon The Tree of Knowledge. Around its stem lesser creatures are assembled amongst luxuriant foliage. All the figures are in deep relief and the quality of the work suggests 17th century origins . . .*

*ibid*

The old lady was a stick of a thing with laboured breathing, but she began by reading stories to Fay – or picking out the thorns from one her many detours into the bramble patch. One morning she undid the child's heavy plaits and redid them to perfect symmetry and, Fay proving amenable, it became a regular thing.

Increasingly Mr Sobel entered into the novel atmosphere. Older than his wife and not much bigger, he had more life in him. His laughter was the loudest noise Mortlake ever heard. Now Mr Sobel produced lozenges of silver foil from his pocket, unwrapping them to reveal white chocolate hearts. Soon he graduated to hiding them whenever Fay was expected. Under the atlas was favourite or the cigarette box that sat beneath the carved owl. Sometimes the search turned into a farce, Mr Sobel falling onto the floor to stare up the flue, jumping onto a stool to check the topmost shelves or behind the gloomy paintings while Fay took every cushion off every chair until only Mrs Sobel was left perched on her sofa, giggling, wheezing, 'No! No! I don't have it here,' as her breath gave out. All this was watched by Hatty. With a child's instinct, Fay recognised competition.

Mortlake's flock of waterfowl threatened to become a flashpoint. These were a mixture, domestic geese mainly, with clipped wings, and a few tame mallards, easy-going on the protected water. Even a pair of swans was not too proud to turn up at the kitchen door on clown's feet. In as much as the birds were anyone's, they were Hatty's. Hatty's appearance on the terrace created a mass exodus off the surface. Hatty prepared and distributed the warm mash from an immense breadcrock as the highlight of their existence. What Fay really longed to do was take the ladle and fling out the food herself in spatters of meal that would send the fowl into a frenzy of drunken combat. To decide where and when the manna landed, that was what she craved. She would never say, but hung around at each opportunity, her eyes flicking from the steaming bran, the ladle, the flock and back to the hand that orchestrated the scrum. Hatty knew. Hatty wouldn't offer. But of course during one library session Fay, doll-like and malleable beneath the caress of Mrs Sobel's own silver-backed brush, did ask. Had the answer ever been in any doubt? Next morning Fay fed the geese . . . and the next, until she grew bored and found something more important to be up to when they arrived.

But it was the chameleon that was Fay's undoing – and her mother's.

The Sobels' money 'came from *abroad*, came from

chocolate' her mother told her, enough in itself to make it the stuff of fantasy. So when they arrived to find an unfamiliar car on the gravel and a stranger at Mortlake, a thin young man in a light suit with skin tanned caramel, it was easy to connect both things. Certainly he looked the part, a traveller from the land of chocolate. He had brought a present for Mrs Sobel. Though who knows how – or for how long – it was meant survive, it was a chameleon. Fay was summoned by a tight-lipped Hatty to see.

The thing was delicate – fabulous . . . not real until it swivelled one bulging orbit in her direction. Fay missed the word they called it by, but knew immediately that here was a dragon in waiting.

For her delight the living jewel is brought up close, balanced on its new owner's palm – where it seems to blanch. The visitor suggests the sombre silk curtains are tried next but, 'Oh, Fay must hold it if she wants to,' Mrs Sobel insists. With great care the exhibit is transferred back to the young man's fingers (each of the legs it raises quickly and independently) but before it has a chance to even think about darkening, the chameleon is placed on the wool of her cardigan.

In Fay's mind she still sees the tiny body become opalescent, a thing of mottled *eau-de-nil* and now mauve, still hears Mrs Sobel crying out, 'Look, it really does change colour – and straightaway,' and Mr Sobel's crumpled-newsprint face beams. Are chameleons anything near so responsive? Or are the years playing her false, Fay wonders? Yet nothing dislodges this scene's minute detail.

'A baby dragon,' Fay calls it. And Hatty is staring neither

at the chameleon nor at anyone else in the room but at a spot far beyond – until the child names the creature and something pent up comes bursting out as, 'Don't be silly! There's no such thing as dragons!'

Fay wants to say, 'There are. My Daddy says Welsh dragons are hottest of everything – you can make toast on their burp.' But the reminder of her father causes a brace of big fat tears to accumulate and come splashing down onto her sleeve and its passenger.

Sometimes when she retells the story to herself the accompanying wail is hers – but sometimes it is Mrs Sobel's. The expression Hatty turns on her never varies.

Her mother wouldn't speak about what got her sacked. In the first chill of Autumn they cycled home for a final time, her mother jerking the handlebars to avoid entire branches torn away by a recent storm. Usually they would sing until the first incline – not 'that pop' which both her parents had been too old to take to, but novelties such as 'Lily the Pink' and 'Two Little Boys', her mother doing the choosing, Fay joining in.

'School's starting soon anyway,' her mother muttered and then stayed quiet. Once away from the trees the westerly wind must have turned her mother's old machine to lead judging by their slow progress. It froze the child's face the instant she raised it from its tucked position against the rough coat. She felt but couldn't hear her mother's sobs. At the ascent into the village and without warning her mother jumped off and pushed, the seat over the back wheel bumping in and out of every rut in the lane, the child chilled and fretful, wanting to complain until a look at her mother's reddened eyes and working jaw silenced her.

When, almost grown-up, Fay asked her, just casually, not making a big thing out of it *What really happened?* she got a garbled reply that ended in 'which I *never* did. I never did.'

A valuable lesson, though, for future writing: not that certain places can be as vital as the people living in them. Other locations, towns, cities and then *abroad* – even as far as the land of chocolate – would teach that. As her readers know, Fay Blethyn finally settled in Paris, in the Ninth Arrondissement, which has also featured in her fiction and where she remains. Neighbours who catch sight of her shopping in Galleries Lafayette or maybe in the Rue Vignon lunching with Isaac Demarais, her husband, believe her to be *une bonne Parisienne.* And her last visit to this area was for her mother's funeral, one bleak January day when Mortlake's continuing existence never entered her mind, nor that Hatty Harris must be long dead. But what she learned from Hatty has stuck. It was the importance of choosing early on just who your main character is. Don't waste your effort along the sidelines. Stick with him – or her. Beady-eyed as a goose, watch for and anticipate her every move and however seductive the others, forget them. Cosset and coddle *her* until she does what you need. In Mortlake's next incarnation, for instance, Fay has decided a woman very like Hatty will –

Something involving water and a bizarre accident, probably. There's plenty of scope with that swimming pool, the lake . . . its spongy bottomed boat.

# BARLEY ROGERS

The roasting meat did it.

No – it wasn't the meat. Barley's stomach had been playing up before Pauline put the birds in the oven. Three chickens, Bonner's best: he'd collected them on his way home yesterday, walking into the yard from around the side of the red-brick house, thinking as he always did how from the front you'd never know someone was running a poultry farm. The other end of Offa's Terrace butted up against a garage with a dozen nearly new 4x4s under a bill-board offering credit. It was owned by Barley and he'd just locked up and set the alarms, as he did six days a week. Across the road St Luke's, the chapel he and Pauline had married in, now offered used office furniture and recondi-tioned laptops. But the only hint of commerce about the Bonners' was on the front wall, a homemade sign they kept getting letters from the Enforcement Officer over, Free Range Eggs and Fresh Chickens. Once up a path flanked by currant bushes, ignoring Elsa the GSD who barked but had arthritis, you found a strip of garden spreading out to a couple of acres. It was surrounded by tin-sheet and larch fencing and stretched behind the houses and all the way back to a branch line, made invisible by hawthorn grown into trees. Either Freddy or Mo Bonner was usually doing something out here, Freddy nailing roof-felt back onto a hen-house or Mo sitting in a plastic chair plucking while the rest of the flock beyond the wire rooted and scratched, unconcerned by feathers from an ex-hen rising with the dust.

Mo Bonner had heaved herself up and brought his order out in a Bargain Booze carrier – so chill it felt like lumps of ice on a warm summer evening. 'Here you go, Barley, dressed and chopped through like Pauline said.' She thrust the note he offered into the pocket of her straining overall, not bothering to look. Collapsed back down, she reached again for the part-downy corpse. 'You got your girls coming tomorrow?'

He nodded, edging away from Mo's big pink legs that had shot out as she landed. 'Yes. Mair-Anne's still in Bangor. She'll bring Jenny with her. Donna and her husband come on the train. Pauline's picking them from Wrexham.'

'O-oo. Dinner's down to dad, is it?'

'Barbeque. Chief cook and bottle-washer, that's me,' he laughed. Then he was out, before they got into *and they'll be bringing the new baby! Elizabeth they're calling her, Pauline said. Nice old-fashioned name . . .*

'Why Barley?' Eugene Rae, before he was his son-in-law, had asked this straight out the first time they met.

At six foot four the young West Indian towered over Barley. But the flat Midlands accent he'd acquired, which turned Barley into *Barlay*, was unsuited for intimidation. Even if Eugene's nature had leaned that way . . . and Eugene's nature couldn't have leaned any further from that way. He was genial to the point of annoying, allowing Barley's bossy youngest daughter to order his life, his home and now the timing of his child's arrival. Elizabeth Rae had entered this world four weeks ago on a fine June night so that she could be settled into her well-researched nursery before the end of the next tax-year. Donna, at twenty-six, was just qualified in accountancy. 'Dad's real name's John,' Donna had butted in as though that were the end of it.

'Barley because I grew up in a pub, The Brickmakers. In the town, bottom of the hill – it's gone now. I'd nick a few measures out the gin bottle and lace Robinson's Barley Water with it. Then I'd take it with me to camp.' Things he hadn't thought of for years came rushing back with the name of the pub: the fierce shine of its façade, for one, glancing off those perfect courses of Monk and Newell reds that in the wet turned the colour of bruised grapes. Above the door had been a terra cotta plaque showing poor labourers stacking bricks in a field, Hope Mountain at their back. In the next panel a fat man in a stove-pipe hat stood between brick gateposts, thumb tucked into his waistcoat. There had been a cane in the other hand – of course, once the whole area had been famous for its kilns and when he was a boy, old people like Keir Williams could pick out a buff Ponkey or a Wyndham brown from across the street, pointing with a finger that had lost its tip in the tile-press. He would tell Eugene about Keir –

But, 'Camp?' Eugene asked.

'Scouts. I was a Boy Scout.'

'Me too.'

Barley lay beside Pauline in the dark after Eugene

and Donna had left. All the excitement of finally having a wedding to plan – three girls, the eldest over thirty now and *at last* a real wedding – was still tingling in her veins. He could feel it. He'd said to her. 'I like Eugene.'

'Of course,' she'd murmured, the bed creaking as she tossed and turned, her brain already at work on lists and venues, 'how could anybody not like Eugene?'

Today the weather was going to do them proud. Morning haze had lifted off the top of the mountain, so restoring the familiar curve of its backbone. The garden, his garden, relied upon it for completeness. From the crazy paving the view was of a perfect, weed-free emerald lawn that swept up to the herbaceous border, a boiling riot of daylilies, *Antirrhinums* and *Crocosmia lucifer* at the moment. Topping them was the pergola Barley had built. It ran parallel to the fence panels and was draped in the clematis Bees Beauty just at its pink-flowered height. Moonlight, the hybrid musk rose, was waiting to take over. At the back of all this, once, had been a silver birch put in twenty years ago by the developer of their small close and chopped down by Barley ten years ago despite Pauline's protests. Hope Mountain, a mile and a half to the west, now drew the eye, trees, gorse and rough pasture, not a mountain in the strict sense, but above it there was only a soaring sky –

Barley's entire length of gut seemed subjected to a rapid descent.

He put a match to his paper and kindling arrangement in the barbeque, a lattice of charcoal onto that and walked back into the house for the fork, tongs and water spray, almost colliding with his wife. She had changed and was in search of car keys.

'You're looking nice.' She was. No longer slim and nearer sixty than fifty, she dressed accordingly, never bulging out of skimpy things the way he noticed some women did, especially in summer, Mo Bonner for one. Today Pauline was in loose trousers and a sort of tunic affair patterned with soft fawn blotches like a tabby's fur. Her round face, which seemed to him never to have aged, was freshly made-up and her iron grey hair neat from its recent trim. 'Bit early, aren't you?'

'I don't want them waiting in the heat, not with Elizabeth.' She might have said 'the baby' but unlike Barley, Pauline had gone to the hospital in Birmingham the day after the birth. She and her granddaughter were familiar. 'The chicken's cooked through so you can put it on at the end to brown a bit more.' She licked the pale pink from her lips in concentration. 'Leave the steaks in the fridge till wanted. Don't go getting out a load of sausages. They only burn and go to waste. If that other pair get themselves here, have them carry stuff out and set the table.'

That he'd do it himself the moment she left, they both understood. He was about to say something but she gave him a peck just beside his eye and was gone. The Meriva's engine started up on the drive. A good steady note: he was ever alert for misses and vibrations and there were none but he wished he'd got her the diesel now. Then he took a first load of the solid earthenware they kept for outside, placing it on the trestle table (his paper-hanging table) already put up on the patio. Pauline had draped it with overlapped cloths, weighted down with serving utensils, though there wasn't a breath of wind. He counted out plates, large and small, six of each. But instead of returning for another load, Barley found he'd sunk onto the low brick wall that kept the grass and crazy paving apart. As he watched smoke oozing from the shiny new barbecue, his insides twisted at the thought of food being cooked, of having to eat . . . he had always had a touchy digestion, even as a boy. Trouble at The Brickmakers, on either side of the bar, or a class test and his stomach went into its own misses and vibrations. Always had. It kept him thin. Once and only once, in front of a couple they were friendly with, Pauline put it down to being allowed drink at too young an age, which was reasoned, not disloyal – but also a dig at his mother and father whom she had never taken to. Usually she laughed off his *not feeling like much* with *lucky you!* or a reference to hot weather, never the past again.

. . . it had been boiling that day too, with an intense bone dryness that you didn't get in Wales, not even here, inland. Nor a sky blue as the candy wrapper in his hand and cloudless because there were no hills within a hundred miles, making it immense. Smoke columns rising straight up from the cook-out were the only verticals to catch the eye. The gleaming steel half-drums were the size of coffins, the sizzling meat in endless spitting rows . . . *Camp?* Eugene had asked. *I was in the Scouts,* he'd answered. And that afternoon he was surrounded by their green uniforms.

He'd been out of the country only a half-dozen times since, always to Spain and with no great pleasure. But at fifteen, a small skinny kid from the local pub with parents who only ever managed a day trip to the coast, was it any wonder America had had the effect it did? It still seemed like a delusion, even now: another version of him who boarded a plane that might as well have been a rocket ship and landed in New York en route for Spokane. He had stood at the top of the Empire State Building with a dozen others and four Scout leaders and a ginger boy from Cardiff – he'd find out was called Dougie – had looked at him, the amazement on his face reflecting Barley's own and said, 'It's good this, innit?'

And later, in South Kansas City, Missouri, Barley had ridden in a Cadillac.

1967 was the year of a World Jamboree. After Idaho – in Barley's memory, one enormous forest – Welsh Scouts went on for a week in Kansas City and found themselves distributed in singles or pairs amongst the giant-windowed homes of doctors, lawyers and ophthalmologists whose boys, *you betya*, were all in the local troop. Barley was billeted on the Alink family of Avondale: Mom, radiologist Dad, and Chuck and Ricky. They were –

*He was fifteen! He'd been to London with the school once, had camped on local farms and in spruce plantations, had earned badges for ropecraft, woodcraft, cooking and astronomy . . .* At the Alinks there was his own bedroom for the first time in his life – a real room off Dr Alink's den with a divan under a Stars and Stripes cover and prints of buffalo and bear and a special lamp for reading in bed. There were *two* inside bathrooms with showers in kiosks made of smoked glass. Barley had never entered a house where everything, from the door handles to the gadget for whipping up milk shakes, looked brand new and worked.

Dr Alink was nearly bald and laconic in speech, Mrs Alink was willowy and pretty and, to be honest, knocked his own mother into touch with her perfect teeth and tight-fitting slacks. Chuck – no threat as a freckled, open-faced thirteen year old, interested in soccer, willing to look up to Barley if only Barley hadn't been a couple of inches shorter than himself. The problem was Ricky.

After the Alinks, along with all the other families, collected Barley at the airport they drove to a diner where the world's largest rack of beef ribs was put in front of him. Was he intended to carve and share it out? Then everyone else's order arrived and only Ricky seemed to guess, his square face turning ugly in a grin. At seventeen Ricky's upper lip and chin were already fuzzed with bronze hair and he was tall as his father. He had the biggest hands Barley had ever seen; Dr Alink caught Barley looking and got Ricky to put one down on the table where it outdid even his own in length and width. Dr and Mrs Alink laughed. Ricky's party trick. All through that first meal he watched Barley's attempt to chomp through enough beef to feed a Welsh family – and every now and then, when his parents weren't alert, he winked. It wasn't friendly.

Avondale, their next stop, was a just-made place of wide front lawns and no walls or hedges. Yet inside the Alinks' house was a formality completely alien to Barley's experience. The boys called their own father *Sir* and even on occasion called Mrs Alink *M'am* although only when Dr Alink was in earshot. Every meal began with grace and to leave the table needed permission. Home must feel more like school to Ricky and Chuck, he decided. Eating fish-fingers between two slices of bread while your dad railed *I'm gonna bar that bloody Keir Williams next time 'e does it* and you tried to watch 'Dr Who' was impossible to imagine. But in private Barley soon found Ricky was a real shocker.

'Here he is!'

His eldest daughter's voice made him jump. The next moment Mair-Ann and Jenny had him between them, their scent enveloping him and Mair-Ann's wild hair in his mouth. 'Come on, you old slacker,' she said pulling Barley to his feet.

Barley put an arm around both and gave them a squeeze of equal force but it was to his eldest his eyes strayed. She was the image of his wife. She was even beginning to add weight, rounding out in the precise way Pauline had. He'd put that down to the three babies in six years. Mair-Ann's hips, exaggerated by a full, long skirt, said he had been mistaken. Her cheek laid itself along his for a long instant – then, 'Ro would've liked to have come,' she said. 'You know – get a look at the first Rogers grandchild – but we can't leave the dog.' Rhona was her co-worker in the University records office, a woman with whom she shared a house. If Rhona had been invited it was news to Barley. Pauline again: she had a way of stepping over things he might have wanted to discuss, pulling rank because *they're girls, Barley.* He could script another of their midnight exchanges, *Mair-Ann talks about this Ro a lot,* his suggesting. *I know – sounds nice, doesn't she? Nice and sensible.*

Jenny was already looking at the table, sizing up the event. Physically she favoured the Rogers' side: narrower, bird-boned in comparison to Mair-Ann and, when Donna arrived, would be dwarfed by her. With a sudden, slightly crooked smile, Jenny could definitely become the prettiest of the three, large-eyed, very vivid. She was throwing herself away in Barley's opinion on a married man still half-living at home with his wife and child. *She won't want to hear it, whatever we think.*

'Champagne is it, Dad?'

'Well I've got the glasses out. Your mum doesn't really like – It's only Cava.'

'Good. I'd rather have it.'

He was in the presence of both girls after a few weeks' absence. Feeling their warm familiarity against his sides and continuing to feel it even when they'd moved off, one wandering the lawn, the other into the house, his stomach seemed to benefit and grow calm. It led him to believe everything was going to be all right. No need to talk about things, Ro or anything else. Just to see and hear the girls – well, it was enough to remind him of his undeserved luck, marrying wisely and being their father. If his stomach complained perhaps it feared disclosure, how one day he'd be found out and it all be taken away

By Pauline's return, a double beep signalling it, Jenny had the table finished and Barley, apron on, was tending the fire. First of the visitors to come out was Eugene, striding to meet him dressed in sober trousers and a light cotton shirt as though for church. Of course it was for church. Eugene sang in the choir. This had delayed their depar-

36

ture from Birmingham and for this reason they would be lunching at nearly half past three. As he always did, Eugene insisted on shaking hands but shyly, looking at Barley's fist inside both of his own, rather than into his father-in-law's face. The sun's glare turned Eugene's glasses into twin mirrors anyway. 'Well, where is she?' Barley demanded, more impatient-sounding that he felt because Eugene would expect it.

'The aunties've got her,' Eugene grinned. '*You*'ll be lucky to get a look-in.'

'How is she – how's being a dad?'

'Righteous! Slept all the way through to the four o'clock last night. Pauline said Donna was the best baby – but I think this one *might* be better.' Eugene was about Donna's age but always seemed younger to Barley, his expression boyish, even when comparing notes on fatherhood.

'Nice work, Eugene.'

'She even slept on the train.'

'You'll need to let me look out for that car now. I've got a Renault Scenic coming in this week, registered 2005 *but* only 15,000 on the clock and that's *kosher*. The woman had it on the forecourt and I took one look and –'

'Donna says *no* – while we're in the centre. Parking at the flat's . . .' He shrugged.

'What about you?'

'I can cycle to the office – ten minutes, max.'

Eugene worked as a debt counsellor – somewhere in the city. One thing was certain: Pauline with Eugene seated beside her, Donna and Elizabeth safe in the back, would have driven past the garage and its newly erected bill-

board. CALL IN FOR OUR NEW DEALS! SIX MONTHS
INTEREST FREE. 'If you just put your hand down behind
that cloth,' Barley suggested, 'I've got beers in the cooler.'

They clinked brown stubbies from a local brewery
with a picture of the near skyline on the label: Hope and
Glory. And Eugene said, 'Hey, that's *not* a bad bitter, that's
*not*.' After a pause, he said, 'I see our pace bowler carved
through Glamorgan – again.' Eugene had a season ticket
to Edgbaston; following Warwickshire was his second religion. '*Yow* Welsh want to give up cricket.'

And after agreeing, Barley could think of nothing else to
do except rest his buttocks against the wall and trace the
line of Hope Mountain with the neck of his bottle. 'Well,
they said it was going to be hot.'

At Swope Park, Kansas City, *29th largest municipal park in
the U.S*, six square miles basked in continental heat. With
air so clear, objects seemed to be edged in black. People's
outlines remained sharp though the figures themselves
flared up with colour wherever you looked. That was
another thing, the flashiness of the clothes, reds, blues and
an alien mustard gold that men, even men in their gardens
on Welsh Sunday afternoons say, were never seen in. And
shorts. Being a Scout wasn't a handicap nor cause for deri-
sion in Swope Park because men wore shorts.

The golf course, a polo field, swimming pools, a zoo, a
lake, an open-air theatre and the Hillcrest Country Club of
which all the host families were members, was to provide
the treats for their guests. Withered grass stretched to the
horizon dotted with clumps of trees of identical height

and girth. There were hundreds maybe thousands in the park but Swope absorbed and distributed them evenly. Wandering in it with Chuck, listening to Chuck prattle on about Coach Muller – how he was never gonna make the swim team like Ricky had – Barley had a piercing sense of removal and sadness. It was the last day – which seemed ridiculous. America was too heated, too much itself, too drastic ever to let him go . . . First he was back in the diner with the Alinks, his face all stiff and hard from not finding a comfortable expression. Dr Alink's pink head, Mrs Alink's blonde helmet of hair, Chuck's metal-braces grin, Ricky's hooded eyes, each reflecting the brilliant strip-neon. A giant rack of ribs mocked him . . . then he was in the room off the den, struggling with a lamp coming out of the wall above his bed, a lamp that swivelled and flexed in so many dimensions, every time he caught it by mistake he thought it broken. The Jamboree Camp back in Idaho was real – and real, raised American voices were shouting 'OK you guys now today we'll hit the trail,' and the horses and bulls at the Boise rodeo were grunting their distress. Now – all still happening. This second.

But home, The Brickmakers' ale and onion atmosphere, a public bar so dark the sun never penetrated and the unvarying cool of its cellars, was like something read about – or had had described to him maybe, but never experienced.

'Let's take a hike!' Dr Alink in a UKC sweatshirt and cap was piling on the enthusiasm now the end of the week was in sight. At his side Mrs Alink, slim as a girl in white culottes, showed even more of her apricot legs. Barley and

Chuck were in full Scout's uniform. Ricky was not, making an obvious thing of detaching himself from his clustered friends to join the trek around the lake and giving a sign behind his back Barley saw. The sun blazed. The packed earth and seared grass beneath their feet felt, to Barley, as if it could ignite without a spark. Yet the offer of 'a couple of innings of softball' from the Browders – Avondale neighbours – was received with extra whooping and horseplay by Dr Alink, causing Barley to wonder if he'd been at Ricky's pills. The Browder father, tall and rangy, was another doctor, his three sons were tanned beanpoles and his party included a burnt ginger Dougie from Cardiff who nodded to Barley. 'Bit like cricket – nah, more like bloody rounders, this,' he muttered. They watched the two fathers draw a diamond in white sand that the Browders happened to have in their station wagon together with wooden bats. The Alinks came up with a rubber mat which was also necessary and Dr Alink said, 'Pitching forty feet?' and both doctors laughed.

Dr Browder countered with, 'Bunting not allowed.'

Barley had to have softball rules explained twice by Ricky and Chuck and again when they walked away by Mrs Alink, who was on their team. But the more they talked at him, the less like cricket or rounders it became. Ricky, after two *balls* – which meant the opposite, no balls – scored a home run. Mrs Alink was surprisingly fast between bases and was almost out by overshooting. Last in, Barley was tagged on his way to second base by Dr Browder who threw with a wild and maniacal expression more frightening even than the projectile aimed at his Barley's heart.

Though not more frightening that Ricky's glare. They hadn't done well. The two men exchanged jokes, but low and not for sharing, while towelling themselves. Mrs Alink, still fresh-looking, waggled a finger at Chuck for some misdemeanour Barley missed. Waiting for Dr Browder to receive Ricky's first pitch, Dougie confided in Barley that he never wanted to go back to Cardiff, could stay in Kansas for the rest of his life as far as he was concerned. Dr Browder only made it to first base but his family yelled as though he'd scored a penalty from the spot.

The game became increasingly shambolic once an audience gathered, yet more doctors by the way they called out things that made no sense to Barley but the fathers found humorous. Dr Alink tripped and rolled in the dust and Dr Browder sprinted over, shook his head and pretended to shoot him, to hoots and groans. Mrs Alink called, 'OK, boys!' in a special, unnatural voice and meaning *not OK boys* like *ball* meant no ball. Dougie, wet hair turned dark and his Scout shirt olive, was tagged by Chuck and kept going anyway while everyone shouted abuse.

Browder Boy number three was maybe twelve – he could have been as old as that. But his hit was a clean *click*. Barley's fumbled clutch as the ball whizzed past his ear gave the Browders victory – and Ricky's 'Aw Jeez you little runt!' caused Dr Alink to suggest he and his elder son go for sno' cones and a talk, even though the smell of fat on charcoal was apparent and Scouts were wandering past holding chicken drumsticks by their burnt knuckle-ends . . .

He was dreaming that last night down next to Dr Alink's

den: he dreamt of Swope Park and sitting at a picnic table, gin and Barley Water in a pint glass, slipping down nicely. And a smiling Mrs Alink beside him picked at a piece of meat, delicately, like a robin pecks a worm, her parted legs coppery, aglow from a set sun . . . He'd been so deep in sleep, Ricky must have had trouble rousing him, even with the torch. Then, 'Shaddup!' Ricky hissed at Barley's first attempt at speech.

'What's the time?'

'Who cares. D'you wanna see something? 'S'up to you.' The beam flicked toward the door and Ricky's sneakered feet walked into it and through into his father's domain.

Barley's watch said gone eleven. In the den the flashlight slithered around and was suddenly straight in his face, Ricky invisible behind it. 'Right – just –' His eyes pained him and he formed the words, the words were there ready to come out *fuck off, Ricky!* 'Hold on,' he said.

It was an old Cadillac they had parked three doors down with the jet plane styling, before they clipped the wings, and whitewall tyres to match the bodywork. Room enough to seat five across the front seat, having no gears, still a novelty to a boy whose father drove a Morris with flag indicators. At first Barley thought maybe the car was all there was.

'Get in.' The way Ricky's two friends looked at each other and sniggered as they'd sniggered at Ricky's sign earlier on, told him it wasn't all.

*Just a drive.* The back rattled with cans. He found he was up against the door, digging into the door with the whole of his body rather let himself touch Ricky's bulk. But there was nothing he could do when the beer exploded all over him as Ricky meant. He took it, gulped. *Gnat's piss.* He was fully awake only now, the liquid welcome in his mouth. *You should try Wrexham Lager and – and a couple of shots to follow it up.*

The tension inside Ricky was like a live thing until he laughed and said, 'Right, kiddo. You can *drink.*' As Barley watched he chose a couple of pills from the palm of his hand and washed them down, handed some across to the Cadillac's driver and co-pilot who swallowed them without looking and offered the last to Barley who couldn't refuse. 'Barley – *ma'man*! S'why we thought you'd like a trip to The Yards.'

And one of the others – what they were called he didn't take in though Ricky told him – said, 'Yeah, Barley. We couldn't let you go back to Wa-ales without a drive by The Yards.'

The Cadillac *pur-rr-ed.* He had never known such a frictionless ride – a glide – so that every part of his body began to feel smooth in sympathy. They were out of Avondale before he noticed, along the North Oak Trafficway which he had been on in the daylight. Then across the ASB bridge, a first.

He would always know exactly where he'd been. Not as it was happening – for now fixing his attention on an object, any object, made it grow until it filled his vision. Though he felt he was seeing it *really* well, to look at the next thing required closing the eyes, starting again. But when he was back up in the attic at The Brickmakers he shared with his brother he spread the Kansas map out on the cold lino and like a good Scout traced their route. Often. The highway was all theirs. The City Stockyards and the West Side Feedyards lay either side of the river, also either side of the state line separating Kansas, Missouri from Kansas, Kansas. And people lived here in houses that were anything but houses. Shacks. They made him think of allotments with their make-do constructs. Single storied as in Avondale, but their porches sagged like The Brickmakers' overloaded cellar shelves. Parked cars were big as the Caddy and suggested affluence until you noted a bonnet removed or blocks for wheels. Even in the shadows the peeling white paint was obvious and where a picket fence survived it was with missing pickets and no gate.

The road they came in on was concrete.

'We'll give our guest the tour!' Ricky crowed and the driver seemed to know what was wanted. He spun the wheel hard. Once away from the main drag, the side street was just dirt, brutal to the Cadillac's suspension and must be what was causing Barley's sickness. Back up into his throat it came, chicken, hot dogs and mayonnaise *like pus* according to Dougie . . . the only thing America got wrong. Barley squeezed his lips shut, felt the world spin and focused on newspapers lying along the road edge as though a newspaper van had crashed and plastic sheeting, everywhere plastic sheeting, discarded in the gutters, in rolls lying on paths and porches. Who could need so much plastic – and for what?

'You really wanna see something, Barley?' Ricky almost whispered.

'Sure.'

'He said *sure!* How about that?' No one laughed now but it couldn't have been worse than this quiet 'Barley says *sure.*'

The car had pulled up. Its massive bonnet poked into a long shallow decline, narrower than any street they'd been on yet and with houses even smaller and more tightly packed. Inside, Ricky and friends *breathed*. Here was even less in the way of lighting though many of the cabin doors stood open and glimmered, as did the porches with hanging strings of bulbs as though for Christmas. There were fewer cars parked leaving room, just, for a single vehicle to pass between them. Could he say *No, I don't want to see something?* On the steering wheel the driver's fingers beat a rhythm against its leather sleeve. 'Ha-ng-g on,' Ricky drawled and flicked on the internal light. From under the dashboard, he produced a steel catapult laced with thick rubber. Barley had never seen one that was not home made before but this was machined. The boy next to him leaned down into the blackness at his feet and said, 'You got BB-guns where you come from?'

Barley nodded yes at the big airgun. They loaded both from their pockets, a glass marble for the catapult, lead pellet for the gun. 'Time to move,' Ricky said. He and the other passenger clambered over Barley, out and into the back seat. Both doors closed with hardly a sound.

'OK?' the driver said. Every light on the Cadillac was extinguished. Even with the windows down it was unbearably hot and they filled it with their smell, sweaty and soapy at the same time and the hot dog grease that was under that. 'OK,' the driver said again but only for himself. He lifted the handbrake and rolled down the slight incline, almost silently. But once level with the first house he revved the engine. In the back Ricky and friend fired, the car bucked forward and they reloaded and fired again into the nearest windows of the next houses and the first cars – and on as they went; cars were favoured as nearer targets. They travelled the street length, with Barley not being able to help himself but crane to see if they were finding their marks though each *whang!* and each shattering of glass was being greeted by *Yeah!* With the Cadillac's wheels screaming against something low and solid, they turned, revved, began yelling *come on out niggers!* and *wake up boy!* then roared back up the hill as shapes moved on the porches and a baby screamed. Just as they were breasting the rise, there was a noise like a shot. Something hit the rear window. 'Shit!' Ricky said. 'They got us. A rock – yeah, a rock.' And the other boy said. 'I think it's cracked, Karl,' at which Karl, the driver, started to curse repetitively under his breath. They took a left – another left and were back on the concrete highway, making for the bridge. But Barley was crouched down in his seat, seeing nothing and nobody, though staring forward into the cone of light. Saying nothing.

What about Ricky? Barley rehearsed Dougie asking the question on the plane and his answer, never needed. Oh Ricky was terrified his Dad would find out he'd been with the guys in the Caddy, Barley would say, Ricky was near pissing himself by the time we crept back in.

'Elizabeth Rae, here's your granddad,' Donna said.

Barley watched her stepping carefully over the paving in strappy sandals that looked as if they needed concentration to keep on her feet. She was wearing a polka dot dress he remembered from her pregnancy, belted now to give a bit of a waist, the eighteenth birthday locket dangling in the V of her neckline as it always did – but her face . . . everything was changed in his daughter's face. That was what he noticed. Every feature was more definite and seated. It was fuller, her habitual frown all smoothed away – there was a new softness, not just of unplucked brows and lack of make-up. From mulish teenager to mother: once she'd shouted *you think you know everything, you* when told she'd regret not trying for university. Now she moved in another sphere, well beyond the reach of his anxieties. What he'd felt and was feeling, independent of his will, he saw was never to be explained – and if it could be, she was untouchable by it. Like trying to throw a hoop around a peg, a game they'd played at Scouts . . . always what he threw would fall short. *I'll admit I was worried about, well, Eugene. Not him. Something – a long time ago . . . there was something happened. I never told anyone, never said. Not him – not Eugene. Me.* 'Asleep is she?' he asked.

'Yeah. They've worn her out in there. So here's Daddy,' she said, having given the impression of not-noticing her husband, 'already on the drink.'

Eugene flinched behind his lenses. 'I've just this minute –'

'And here's Granddad doing the same.' Donna displayed the sleeping baby to Barley within the shawl he'd watched Pauline making all through winter, her painted nails blurring as she weaved. Elizabeth's eyes were screwed up and one pink and golden fist curled tight against an absurdly tiny ear. Her lips suckled in sleep – otherwise she was a fine bone-china doll. 'Who does she look like?'

'Jenny,' he answered without hesitation.

'*I know!*'

Eugene leaned over mother and child and said, 'I was talking as we came up here, Barlay, I was saying they'll have no worries who her daddy is but they *might* want to know who's her mum,' and received a dig in the ribs.

'Well?' Donna said, 'Aren't you going to hold her, Dad?'

He put down the bottle. 'I smell of beer.'

'Yeah. That's something she'll have to get used to.' But she smiled.

Elizabeth was placed into his arms as Pauline arrived carrying a tray of raw sirloin. Jenny appeared with sticks of bread in a basket and wine bottles cloudy with condensation which Eugene relieved her of. She grimaced. 'By the time our Mair-Ann gets here with that chicken Dad'll have the steak done and we'll be onto dessert.'

But any moment now Mair-Ann and the cooked chicken would join them. And Donna, not he, taking charge would pour the Cava, staring hard at Eugene until he said, '*Right* well, everybody – here's to Elizabeth Rae!'

Barley's heart pounded against the weightless bundle, feeling her liveness through his shirt. Such heat and so little of her: both Eugene and Donna tall and big-boned and Elizabeth so small . . . Pins and needles were already in his hands, their proper sensation seeping away along with the strength. He thirsted for the beer that was unreachable now and to sit down, or find the wall again with the backs of his legs, to be able to brace himself against the wall he'd built, even though Elizabeth's weight was nothing.

His stomach winced at its own emptiness and at the milky sweet-sour baby scent and, just for a moment, he felt she was going to drop.

# FALSE BANDED

Bethan braced for Ollie's reply. She had heard it a few times since getting off the ferry at Dun Laoghaire.

'I'm a poet. This is my sort of . . .' pause, 'West Coast Greats tour, yah?' Ollie's long, sensitive hand would be coming up to his high sensitive forehead and then to the spot where future grey would sprout. (Not that it would do him any harm, according to Andrea). Assured of the listener he let his eyes slide to a faraway focus that said *and even as we're having this conversation deep creative stuff's happening. Lucky you.*

Cheerful Mrs Pearson quivered in the full-on beam of charm while still serving Bethan's scrambled eggs which looked today a bit nodular and dull, whereas yesterday Ollie's had been eggy perfection. Mrs Pearson positioned Ollie's porridge before him by cushioning its impact at the point of landing: poetic productivity in no danger of disruption.

'I'll need some more butter, please,' Bethan said. 'Any chance of ketchup?'

Between them was laid out heavy silver cutlery, Llandudno Hotel style, plus plates, dishes on plates, cups and saucers, milk, sugar, juice tumblers – and condiments in male and female ceramics. *A Beth and Ollie parody*, he'd noted. And they were. The salt's fixed smile was topped with a mousy bob, the pepper, all angular and dignified, had a detectible sneer as though daring its use so Ollie came out ahead yet again.

They were the Bed and Breakfast's only guests. Three other white-clothed tables surrounded them, but virginal, in waiting. Apart from Ollie there was nothing else to look at. *Not that it would do him any harm at all.* A spring of dark hair was loose and mobile as he chewed – she had to force her attention away...

Outside Castaways' glassed-in balcony a soft Connemara morning was drizzling up seriously – the Atlantic Ocean, clouds, distant hills all of a consistency. In the foreground was a garden whose only planting of hydrangeas were cauterised and tipped backwards into open fans. Next door, the other side of a chain-linked fence, Renvyle golf links dissolved even as she watched. Warm Wild And Wet the Connemara sign had boasted ... right on the edge of her field of view a man walked quickly and purposefully with neither clubs nor dog for alibi in the direction of the shore. On some sodden pilgrimage of his own no doubt – before she could determine what it was or point him out to Ollie, the mist took him. She poured herself more coffee and slipped the sweater around her shoulders in lieu of saying anything.

Six months ago Ollie had ambled into her bookshop on The Square. His purpose was already decided; he'd come to do a reading. While Andrea, the assistant, made a big thing of

51

getting him a glass of water, spreading books out on the table he'd sit at, Ollie held onto Bethan's hand though he'd finished shaking it. He observed her steadily . . . The only other writers she had met in the flesh had been huge disappointments. A paunchy sports commentator with his autobiography (*Both Thighs Round The Ball*) attracted a decent crowd. They sold three dozen copies, their best ever for a single title and he had been funny but then rude when asked not to smoke in the porch as she was locking up. The second writer was a woman with a child dying from a rare disease. Hampered by nerves she had stumbled over a question, snapped at the questioner believing herself criticised and lost audience sympathy, an embarrassment. It just wasn't the sort of shop or the sort of town where you were going to get Philip Pullman in. This was Dial Green – the Welsh Borders but a long way from Hay.

Then here was Ollie – a local poet but outdoing all of her and Andrea's expectations. Not arrogance, which would never have worked, but attitude, a sort of personal idiom to the way he leaned forward, slouched back, considered with a slight shake of the head before his responses, all seemed to be included in the trick. A bodily performance. Whatever it was, it wound her up. She watched and listened for half an hour and that was it. No pretence even before he was done with the signings: 'That bistro round the corner'll be open afterwards – if you don't have to shoot off.'

*Good moves*, she'd confided next morning to Andrea, *with nothing too imaginative or freaky . . . qual-it-ty!* It had been worth having to drive him home before getting in to work. And many times since – so that she'd learned how he was born only ten miles from the shop, had been to Cambridge (North East Wales Institute for her) and was twenty-seven. (*Ouch,* Andrea said). His mother administered a national drama scheme from Stratford, the father – they were divorced – was a solicitor in Oswestry and Ollie was 'holed up with the old man for the time being.'

Now, together, they were on a tour of writers' hangouts in the West of Ireland: *W.B.Yeats, top poet, John Millington Synge, top playwright, no arguments.* As if she were going to. Not on their first trip. On its opening night in Dublin, they checked into a guest house in Lower Gardner Street that 'someone' had recommended to Ollie. Ollie's speech was shot-through with anonymous someones. A walk to the rebuilt Abbey Theatre and a drink with the poet ghosts at Toners pub – all as expected. As was some nice efficient sex, afterwards . . . *Yeats and his friends got a tart in for the evening and she stood naked in front of the fire and told them this tale about pubic hair* . . . but she never heard it. Just the litter blowing along the gutters outside, gritty and restless and exciting as Ollie made the backs of her shoulders tingle with gentle and less gentle bites. And on the stage of her mind was a counter-Ollie. He lounged fully-clothed in a chair, whisky in hand, exchanging the odd remark with those nameless friends while taking in every bit of her. Very cold, the eyes.

Bethan would have stayed there: four more nights . . . *yes let's do it!* The drive next day to Connemara seemed endless and he hated her music. By Athlone he was sleeping like a child.

Then once at Castaways – another Ollie choice – sex

became leisurely, happening with a new wordiness. *So Yeats – first he's in love with the beautiful Maud and it's a passion that's got to create or kill! . . . it doesn't kill him . . . and then – well, 'There is grey in your hair' – yet he never stops loving her though she puts him in hell and when he falls for the daughter – Maud's illegitimate daughter, yah? – Maud says try your hand – he's coined his heart for her, and she says to him now I can see you with my daughter and not care . . . Iseult, half-French, she was stunning – more a modern sort of look than the mother's. Reminds me of you . . . the lips – especially the lips.* Another night, a different play.

'So where are you for?' Mrs Pearson's blouse had been smoothed and straightened by the looks of it and her cheeks pinked up from the kitchen. She was back with butter, without ketchup. 'Raymond has just had the forecast. It'll be all gone by twelve.'

More weather was rolling in than could be gone by Christmas, surely? Ollie of course was willing to believe. 'Will it? Achill . . . or is that a bit far? We'd need an earlier start?' John Millington Synge, the one she knew something about, the one whose *Playboy of the Western World* she had actually been in at school, had taken a back seat since Dublin. Now he looked like being dropped. 'The Lake Isle of Innisfree, then.'

During the interval in the latest glitzy sex, Ollie, sprawled among thrashed white bed linen, had said a poem. The style was confiding – and nothing to do with Innisfree. *The woman molten eyed dressed me in heat/ and this close moment, sheeted from the next/ ballooned, denying clothes to following dawn./ That night –*

'– then Ben Bulben because an important image,' he was telling Mrs Pearson. 'And we might get to Drumcliff for Yeats' grave.' That voice of his caused some injuries. It had the first evening at the shop – accentless and deep to go with shadows beneath the brow ridges, musical even in speech.

'Just the thing. I've got drop scones coming.' Mrs Pearson seemed to see the pot of butter for the first time and presented it to Ollie. 'You'll manage a couple of them, I'll bet you will.'

When the woman had gone Bethan said, 'It's all outside?' The eggs were dry and refused to be speared by fork. 'In this?'

'You heard her. Fine by lunchtime. It's a drive, anyway. We'll be in the car till then.'

He sprinkled extra Demerara into the steaming oatmeal and added cream until its surface became richly marbled. Delicious: when he plunged in the spoon and carried it to his mouth, her stomach flipped.

By the time they were ready to leave she had jollied herself to the level of hopefulness, then had to go and gun the engine as she saw Ollie's tall, easy-jointed figure appear on the steps and stall. A complete survey of the half-acre of tarmac that was Castaways' frontage was needed before he could make it over to the car. He slipped in beside her, the droplets shining on him and carrying the impression of another conversation just finished – and finished well. 'Where were you?'

'Mrs Pearson . . . she was telling me about Kearney's. We

can't miss Kearney's she said.' He put on a mock-frown. 'It might be a relative.' Then he smiled.

'OK,' she said, defeated, 'which is it first?'

'The Lake Isle.'

'Oh bliss.'

In the car she put on Tracey Thorn's vocal confessionals – her present poison – and had Ollie rolling his eyes at 'Hormones'. She had been warned by Andrea (who worked only part-time because her parents owned a garden centre and paid for treats) about the West of Ireland roads. They were winding and lethal. That Andrea's brother had managed to write-off a new Lexus somewhere south of Limerick may have coloured her judgement, Bethan thought. But no, Andrea was spot-on. The endless lanes had two only aspects. Either they were on this out-of-season weekday, mesmerisingly deserted – or having lulled the driver into this assumption (it happened now) they produced a sudden convoy of very fast on-coming traffic. This one comprised a bread van, an ancient saloon steered by a rough collie until you noticed it was left-hand drive and a pure-white Rolls Royce containing a froth of bridesmaids.

'Only in Ireland!' Ollie was enjoying himself. He had already highlighted a caravan that was in the process of being entombed by breezeblocks into a static building and a row of cottages where the derelict middle one had been painted to match the inhabited ends, with crude children's faces at each boarded up window. She, teeth-gritted, was now forced to back a Fiesta suddenly doubled in length, half-way to Tipperary. If he could have left it at that –

'Only in Ireland –' he had to repeat, 'can they make a line of vehicles into a one-act straight off the Abbey –'

He would have continued with something along the lines of *a Citroen, a bread van and a white Rolls Royce,* jockeying with sound-values and word-order, if she hadn't exploded: 'For God's sake Ollie! We nearly just got wiped out. You'd feel a lot less oh-the-charm-of-it-all if you drove.'

Ollie couldn't drive. His sulk lasted them to the Lough Gill turnoff. No *I will arise and go now . . .*

Suits me, she fumed, following a wooded valley bottom glimpsed through swipes from the wipers. I never said I loved your mind.

The huge smudged lake that had been such a magnet for William Butler Yeats was scenic enough, though no more so than you could find in Wales. The promised island was at least present but when it came down to it, all Innisfree had on offer was to be floating in a wet place under a big bully of a sky. Nor was it the only island out there, something that was vaguely annoying. Gortexed and booted, but holding hands, they strolled through the trees to the little wooden jetty. A sheet of paper had been inserted into a plastic bag and tacked to a post and needed to be shaken out to read: Trips For Lake Isle Stopped Because Of Family Passing On.

'A whole family,' Ollie intoned and she burst out laughing. They wandered the shoreline. 'Quiet, huh? Makes Dial Green . . . Manhattan.' With cloud cover so complete the effect was of weak luminosity from the surface of the water, its source submerged. When she said as much you could see him filing it away and she was gratified. A stray droplet found its way into her clothes causing a shiver at its progress down the neck, onto her spine . . . 'Of course he didn't *really* want to come and live here. Willy Yeats liked his creature comforts – wouldn't have enjoyed fending for himself . . . there's this story about a journalist going to interview him when he was living in the Tower at Ballylee, yah? And all the time they're talking he can see Georgie –

'Georgie?'

'That's the one he married, finally. After Maud – after them all. Hmmm? Not sure why. She did . . . something. So there is Georgie up a ladder arrangement they have rigged up – and she's painting the ceiling. Journo says nothing about it – neither does Yeats. *Anyway,* he wrote 'Innisfree' walking along the Strand in London, saw something in a shop window. It's about the *idea* of escape . . . gets to us all at times. That's how he manages to poke a vulnerable spot and forces us to say *Yes please!*'

Bethan couldn't stop herself wondering what Ollie needed to run from. The job-lite at Radio Wales, one morning a week, and poetry days for school kids? Readings from *The Life Doctor?*

. . . his beautiful hands cradling it, half-obscuring an etching of 'Vesalius the sixteenth century anatomist', reproduced in blood red and run across front and back cover by a female designer – another 'someone'. Its forty-eight pages were perfect bound but with a deliberate sloppiness in the face-trimming and grant-aided, of course and false banded, a printer's trick for offering much and giving least. Ollie, stern in monochrome, sat in a neat box over the ISBN number and price . . . there was some other sort of poet's residency coming along for him to live on next, free money for just being Ollie and giving him 'the time to produce a full collection.' Whereas she loved work, her shop and its demands: the reading group that used it on a Wednesday evening and bought titles *by the shedload*, even the children in fancy dress for Goblin Saturdays. She'd thought she liked books and found she preferred selling them from the patchwork of Andrea's table display, the harlequin tiles of her own newly-done window. Art objects. But whenever she looked at Ollie another part of her – a part not responsible for stock-ordering, staff rota-ing, Orange Prize shortlist featuring – said all that couldn't continue if Ollie were clipped out. It would be bleak.

'Don't look round,' she warned, 'I think we're being watched.'

Of course he did begin to turn. About twenty yards away, under the shelter of an immense hazel coppice, stood a gaunt but upright man. One hand was on a walking stick, the other thrust into his jacket pocket. Haze was around him and his clothes were tailored in fawn/grey suggestive of tweed, blending in. Either he was weatherproofed in some expensive fashion or he was soaked because each of the hazel's round gold leaves was releasing rain once removed. And he was bareheaded, *white*-headed. Old but not it seemed bothered by the elements: in fact sheltering was just what he was not doing. He had stopped in mid-stride to observe.

Abruptly he vanished, presumably down a woodland trail.

'Where?' Ollie whispered just too late.

'Never mind.'

'Well who was it? What did he look like?'

She opened her mouth to speak but shook her head. Impossible to tell now with the air soupy and thick shadows falling across his face. Nor even what he had actually been wearing –

'Definitely . . . getting on a bit,' she told Ollie. She could see his frustration at the lack of anything to go with this, the lack of a picture. Then she said she may have been wrong which pleased him even less.

'Either he was there or he wasn't,' he groused. He switched his attention to the island. That's what he would do – make you earn back his notice. Paint a ceiling. Well that wasn't going to happen. Paint your own ceiling. As they retraced their route she caught herself, though, searching among woods that crowded right up to the runnels on either side of the road for the solitary walker whom she *had* seen. If she could just –

At the car a text from Andrea informed her Buks illegul frm 2day so brnt shop. Contact with the outside world gave a sense of superiority, of her own personal adulthood. She smiled and refused to read it out. 'Sorry about the island. Now I'm looking for?' she prompted, moving off.

'There's the house – Lissadell. Don't know if we can go in,' Ollie admitted. 'But it's where *he* spent a lot of . . . time.'

The rain abandoned restraint, throwing a complete sheet of water over the windscreen. Momentarily there was the impression they had taken a wrong turning, had now plunged back into Lough Gill. 'A house, definitely,' Bethan said. 'Perhaps they'll take pity on us. Give me a town to aim at. Better still give me a road number.'

But his silence and a sideways glance told her he had neither. 'I thought we'd get directions . . . on the boat.'

She slammed on the brakes. In the rear-view she had the satisfaction of seeing the Lake Isle of Innisfree entirely sunk now, cloaked in murk that had a sinister violet heart. Slowly she let her forehead dip until it touched the steering wheel.

'Get it off your phone.'

'It's just my old phone not a Blackberry,' she said, her lips kissing the plastic central logo.

Ollie's phone was never with Ollie. 'Sat nav?'

She sat up. 'Nicked. I told you. The day I took you to Stafford, when we had to – I *told* you.'

'There's always the grave. That's definitely Drumcliff . . . *Cast a cold eye on life on death, horseman pass by.* He wrote it himself, his epitaph –'

'Have you done yours yet?'

But as she drove the snaking miles back to the Sligo road she found herself catching reflections at every turn of her head: Ollie's first, the barely sloping high forehead with its spill of hair, the definite jut of his chin. When he asked if something was up, she realised she had moaned. 'Hungry,' she lied. Next she looked at herself pretending to adjust the mirror. She was *hot* . . . hair sleeked down, the face better post-thirty than with the twenties baby fat still hanging around. Full lips pouted, luscious as Iseult's.

At the crossroads again there were the same half-dozen houses in rainbow colours and Kearney's Bar, a serious puce with mustard for the stone dressings. Now the lights

had been lit against the midday gloom and the door stood
open.

'In?'

'In.'

If this were Kearney himself behind the bar, Kearney the
third according to Ollie, then he was a broad Mrs Pearson
in man's clothes. His rosy skin might never have grown
stubble and the wide set eyes were baby blue. He brought
drinks over with: 'You're after going to the Isle, Una said? I
saw your car earlier.'

'Yes,' Ollie said, 'but it's no way.'

'No, no,' their host agreed.

Kearney's was a pub and more. They were settled with
the few other drinkers in the small lounge-bar from which
could be viewed a front room grocery store and a hallway
tourist information office with a teenage boy tapping on a
laptop. In one dusty alcove between that and a further bar,
a second-hand book sale attracted Ollie instantly. Floor-
to-ceiling shelving was packed with paperbacks. Immediately Bethan picked out the old orange and white Penguins
that said *3/6 Complete and Unexpurgated*. They looked in
mint condition. Ollie turned *Love among the Artists* to face
her with a quizzical look but didn't wait for response –
Shaw was replaced by Flan O'Brien who was immediately
dropped in favour of George Moore's *Confessions of a Young
Man*.

An intimate knowledge of Ireland's writers burst out of
Ollie in a series of quotations which were right up Kearney's street, by the looks of it. Pints were poured. 'I'll have
the crab and my er –' *There's a first*: Ollie stuck for words.

'Bethan you'll have the salmon, is it, yah? Doesn't have to be soon, we're fine. All this is . . . just wicked for me. I'm a poet myself. Ollie Farr Jones. Huh? *The Life Doctor.* Yah, isn't it?'

'The landlord's a reader,' he informed her bringing Guinness and a Perrier.

Bethan sorted leaflets. Yeats' Lake Isle was familiar on one, even in sunlight. The full text of the poem was beneath, the poet's portrait by Augustus John also. There was the Yeats Summer School, ah, and Lissadell, and Drumcliff with its pictured tombstone. (She remembered Andrea's expression when she'd revealed Ollie's invitation to the Greats Memorial Tour and her dismissal of 'You don't go on holiday to look at old bones. Get off to Ibiza!')

'He said the house is a fair drive,' Ollie said.

'I heard.'

'But well worth it.'

'Didn't catch that bit.'

His face froze. Oh it was a good face, despite the horsy length of it, and irresistible. That time in her bookshop when she'd bought four copies of *The Life Doctor* for non-existent poetry-mad friends and taken him home for herself it had been just to keep seeing that face. Just to get a smile from that mouth, the best thing the town had offered *for a bloody long while*. Which is why she'd been slut-easy and why Andrea still seethed.

'We can just do the churchyard,' he muttered. 'It's nearest.'

But the damp and the devil seemed to have got into her. 'I was talking to Raymond this morning – Mrs Pearson's son, Raymond – and he said – he's a bit of a joker I know – but he said it's probably not him in the grave. Not Yeats at all. They had to bury him in France 'cos there was a war on. Then they lost track of who they'd put where – well you would do wouldn't you, with a war going on?' Why was she saying this? 'And so . . . so when they sent the coffin back to Ireland no one was really sure. Might be him. Or it might be some waiter or pastry chef, or –' her imagination dipped surreally on her, 'or a lace-knickers maker . . . ' she trailed off. When the open doorway was filled, they both looked to it.

The hooded figure, tall as a man, stooped to uncover its head. A young woman was not what Bethan was expecting or wanting, a newcomer who swept past them shedding raindrops. She was greeted at the bar – and from shady corners others called out with intonations so powerful Bethan wondered if it were Gaelic. A Welsh speaker, Ollie for instance, might expect to catch a word – but Ollie was fixated on the mass of revealed blonde hair. From beneath a cagoule the newcomer took out a tube of cardboard, the sort of the thing posters arrived in at the shop. From the tube she slid a wooden flute, letting the instrument roll to rest on a table-top and only then shrugging out of her wet things. Ollie abandoned his glass and was up and over there. An instant kill: high, genuine laughter from *her* with a lot of hair shaking, something clipped and inaudible from Ollie that made it happen all over again. A long wait with only the boredom of fizzy water for Bethan, then, 'That's Roisin. She's here for a session,' he whispered. 'Nothing arranged – they're just doing it, yah?'

The big clock behind the bar was showing a quarter to two but it was so black outside now it could have been much later . . . .and around them Kearney's began to fill. Getting on for two on a Friday afternoon in September, along a road that may or may not take you to Sligo, but they came from somewhere. In the gloomy depths a match was put to the fire. Flame shot up beyond Ollie's profile and his skin flushed, handsomely.

He was going to sing. Bethan knew it. He'd made up his mind to sing. He had the voice – and maybe later he would read. No, he would read. There were a few pieces from *The Life Doctor* that could do well here. Short, flashy, funny . . . her least favourites.

Yellow-haired Roisin was preparing, too. She was sipping from a tumbler, one hip against the bar while she exchanged a word now and again with Kearney but surveying the crowd, eyes there, back again . . . twice to Ollie for everybody else's once . . . she was *not* pretty when you became accustomed to the presence of her. A bit of a beaky nose spoiled things. But she was tall and on home ground and very slim under the flowered dress that fell to a pair of shiny black wellingtons. Anticipation was flooding the room; the talk quietened and rose and quietened again, a test of the moment, not wanting to be caught out. Strong white fingers skittered exercise patterns over the tabletop, also testing. Roisin fielded Ollie's look over all of the other assembled heads, complicit.

'So off to this grave, eh?' Bethan teased him.

'No-o.'

On the bar Kearney was now resting a shabby button-accordion. She went to him before he gave up his post. 'A half of Guinness . . . So, Kearney's?' she offered for the wait.

'My great grandfather.'

'And did he know Willy Yeats?'

Kearney's baby-blue irises had huge dark depths. 'Would you think I'd say no? . . . so your man's a poet?'

'Mmm-mm . . . we-ll . . . mm.'

'Yes, yes.'

Something made her run on with, 'Down by the lough – it sounds, well, mad, but I saw this figure. He was a bit ancient – and striking, silver haired, tweedy. Then he was gone.'

Kearney was nodding, 'I know.'

Unexpectedly a stranger, a bartender she had just spoken to for the first time was assuring her that *he knew*. And she believed him, partly because she had no choice, she just did. But also because something unused inside her had been reacting to Ollie's every lift of chin and gesture of hand since they'd rolled into their hard Dublin bed – and there was no turning it off now. Its pilot light offered a flare up even at Kearney, even with his womanly jawline. Those confidential eyes, full of interest and on her. 'And?' she said.

'I know what you're conjecturing – Ah, here you go.' He slid a customer's offered empty under the tap without glancing down, and put a full bitter into the hand while carrying on, 'Catches a lot of them out, he does. To the life, though, isn't he?' Kearney tapped a picture of W.B. Yeats in a line-up of other sepia dead. 'But you've seen Major Dalgleish come down to look at the trout. That's what. Lost his wife a while back and he's filled up with it, you know how it is. Badly. So he won't fish, never again. I think he won't. '

'Oh.' Just a Major Dalgleish, then. For an instant her thoughts muddled up the jetty notice entombed in plastic, the Family Passing that had cancelled their trip – until she dismissed the link. A major and a boat-trip business were incongruent. 'I mean, that's really sad,' she said.

'It is.'

Kearney took a cloth and polished within a millimetre of the two settled halves of Guinness then, taking them up, added to each with a mother's care. He said, 'Willy Yeats, he wasn't up to much till he passed thirty. They say. Give him time and –' Roisin's first half-dozen practice notes sweetened the room and flew away. A woman coughed by the fire, getting it over with and Roisin stepped forward into the space that had suddenly cleared. Kearney winked at Bethan, murmured: *'But O that I were young again / And held her in my arms.'*

Ollie wouldn't be needing that one for years. She could see him from here; heavy lids tightly shut might denote listening: running ahead to his own performance, more like, which would be *so* good –

And because Kearney was Mrs Pearson to a T, a picture of the room, her and Ollie's room at Castaways, shot into mind.

Mrs Pearson is flicking out a new snow-field of sheet across their rumpled bed. The chair in the corner from which Ollie sits watching is turned a degree or so, one more, until it's just right. *I did see somebody,* she would tell him. *Thin in the face – a very definite sort of face even though he was getting on. Like a vision.*

'Give him his chance,' Kearney said.

'Oh, I'm going to.'

# EYEFUL

He was famous – well, if not famous exactly, his picture was up. There was no identification of course. How could they ever have got hold of a name? But he recognised himself straightaway and thought: Get anyone who knew me around that time – not that there's many still about – but get one of them and plant them here and ask 'Who's that, then?' And they'd see the hair all over the face and me looking from under it with the thumbs up sign I used to do – and 'Eryl Bennion' they'd say.

Anyone of them would, for certain.

There was a time he'd been brought here every August and knew it better than home. Off the estate and straight onto the old A541 Chester to Holyhead, with the cases on the roof and the Vauxhall Viva threatening to rattle itself apart – the towns along the road just had to be got through until the marble church poked up in the distance and he knew before it they'd be making a dive for the coast.

Rhyl. If you said you were going to Rhyl in his school it gave the sort of status only Disneyland conferred now. Because there was nothing a child could want that Rhyl hadn't got. It was Christmas morning, Boxing Day and birthdays rolled up into a place and laid out in the heat. Always sunny. That was the deal his memory made with the past; though it can't have been, it was always Sunny Rhyl. Like now. It had drizzled as he was leaving after his wife had gone to work, the one day in the last month he chose to up and go. The few belongings thrown into the boot – a random selection of clothes because he was unused to packing for himself – and he'd accelerated out of the avenue without any idea of where to. An hour later there was the sun beating down on the golden sands, the water which was never clear, not like off Pembrokeshire say or even Anglesey, as nearly blue as strong light and cloudless sky could produce. Though a swim was low on his list of intentions. It was early June and in a couple of month's time would still be chill and not able to tempt him. You needed to be a child again not to mind. And there was also the whole lone skinny man cavorting about in a pair of Speedos thing. It had 'perv written all over it' as his eldest daughter might say. A poor start to a celebrity career, not what he had in mind.

Hanging round getting wasted maybe but not that.

Just being able to drive himself in was a new experience. Uncle Pete used to bring them to be dropped at the caravan site – one of the really cheap ones well short of a seaview. It must've been a mile walk to the beach and the same back all tired on the first day and crabby – that would be his mother and his big sister Bren. And then Pete might disappear all night, only returning for breakfast to a caravan that would ring like an instrument with sobs, threats and tinny clangs. So he drove along the promenade, the windows down and the radio up, trying to isolate the cause of a warmth in his lower chest. It was evasive. It couldn't be the familiar Front itself, which seemed to have nose-dived through seaside tawdriness into squalor and disuse. Nor the bingo callers that hadn't changed at all. It was the sand filling the gutters! He always looked forward to it. A flat town and built up, in many streets the beach was invisible – but the sand was ubiquitous, followed you like a promise, kicked about and traipsed in, saying this is nowhere ordinary. Feel it.

The first shock came next – not *the* shock but a bad one. As Eryl approached the river, and distracted by the new colour of the ironwork bridge it hit him: there was no funfair!

When anyone mentioned Rhyl for all these years he had thought of Ocean Park. But The Big Wheel was gone. The Jet Stream Roller Coaster and the Wilson Orbiter? – sprawling intricate mechanisms and gaudy testaments to excitement – were all missing. From a tailing vehicle he was hooted just for slowing down at the demolition site it had turned into. He parked on waste ground near a deserted Marine Lake and walked back to have a proper look. There were new flats – on a billboard. White and modern they ascended like decks on a ship. A woman approached lugging a shopping trolley – as he stepped off the pavement for her she must have caught his expression. 'Pity eh? All the old fair – Gonna be nice though, isn't it?'

No, he felt like shouting after her, it's not. It's – not that he'd swear at a strange woman, not without reason – fucking not!

They had got rid of the fair. Massive, or it had seemed massive, acres of beating whirling jigging gear. And you could have cut the noise and smells into slices and sold them on a bun. All knocked off the face of the earth. The next person to come along was male – someone he had just watched swinging down from the digger next to the only bit of fair left, scraping it up to go into a skip. Wood, sheet metal and bright orange plastic – nothing recognisable. Cocky as a chimp he looked but he stopped the man. 'When – when did it all go?'

'Last year most of it.' He said, scratching. Not even summer proper yet and his sunburn was severe enough for the inked barbed-wire round his neck to peel. Sunny Rhyl.

'Last year?' Eryl knew he sounded like the woman with the shopping but couldn't believe something so – not just big . . . not just old . . . *major*, that was the word . . . had been flattened. You couldn't get rid of a landmark, surely, as though it were an old garage you were knocking down?

'Last Winter. We started clearing before the frost. Bastard job.'

Uncle Pete would have said Flaming Nora! That was one of the repeatable ones, not that he was a real uncle – and after he had gone they found out he wasn't even Pete.

When there was no reply the man, Digger Monkey he christened him – he couldn't speak to him but could think up a derogatory name – dodged around and set off in the direction of the centre. Leaving the car where it was Eryl gave him a start and did the same. Though checking out the arcades and fuming, It's not the school holidays yet and there's plenty of kids in playing the slots, his main concern was for a pub, somewhere an out-of-towner on his own won't get glassed. But each step further away did nothing to weaken the mind's drag back to Ocean Park.

To Fatima – Queen of the Nile.

At the edge of the fair, away from the rides – and the capering operators that drew Bren – in a thick smog of their exhaust, came the booths and sideshows. The rump of Victoriana, they suggested sleaze. Not that Eryl thought of them this way – they were the forbidden fruits, what you could get hold of once you'd endured the endless running-in of childhood. The digger-driver's tattoos had conjured them up in all their tarnished glamour. There had been a tattooed giant sitting in a hut no bigger than a phone box behind a curtain. The red and blue inked feet, bare and ridiculous, protruded from under – free samples. His toes were the size of fish fingers and each one had its bloody dagger pointing out. Eryl never saw the rest. He refused to spend. Nor on The Living Leprechaun, green and impish in portrait, whose normal-height wife had facial warts and was his barker. Because next door to him was The Most Amazing Spectacle Ever To Come Out Of Africa! See Her Defy Death!! See Queen Fatima Lie Down Amongst The Crocodiles!!! Spread over the shuttering and larger than life lounged a painted Queen Fatima. Pearls hung from jet black hair onto her forehead. The ruby in her navel was half a billiard ball. A veil covered the face apart from a pair of smouldering eyes . . . and one complete breast was just on the point of struggling free and straight onto the head of a crocodile being used as a cushion.

He was in love.

Each holiday he plagued them to be allowed to go in. *No!* Ten pence it started off at – though afterwards the price was raised. On the hoarding beside Fatima's picture where the paint had blistered you could see she'd been a shilling once.

Same thing, son – that was Uncle Pete.

It was Uncle Pete ruined it. A stranger in many ways, he noticed things about Eryl that sailed straight over his mother's head. He wouldn't be around much longer and probably knew it. 'Here,' he said, 'I'm off for a –' he mimed the tipping bottle. 'See you later.' He dropped the boy a handful of coins. 'Go get an eyeful,' and they exchanged a look that said, on Pete's side, I've been there, kid, but there's no telling – you have to do it yourself and then you know.

Eryl clutched the coins until they were welded to his fingers before he found the nerve. Inside was gloomy and you blinked in the dust kicked up by the punters ahead, men and boys as far as he could tell. He had to grope for the rail, his breath coming in shallow gasps while waiting for his night vision. Fatima – so small! – sat on a Persian carpet in a wooden corral lit by Aladdin's lamp. She leaned on shiny cushions, dressed in slave girl pants and ordinary sandals and a gold bikini top that, as he closed on her, revealed something had dribbled down it like ketchup. Each of the trio of crocodiles was stuffed and not that big either. Two were glass-eyed as teddy bears. One, arranged so its snout just rested on the satin knee of the Queen of the

Nile, looked as though it had dozed off through her stroking, which she did now and again.

She was focused regally into the distance and completely still. He and the rest of the fools inching round and
out again could have been invisible. But when she noticed
Eryl she winked and the black kohl points to her eyes wrinkled up. She was old as his gran.

He does the town, remembering it as big. There was
somewhere he never got to in his week. A joke shop that
by the time he found it his holiday money had run out, or
an arcade with the latest monsters covering the windows
seen on the last tired tramp to the caravan before home
– always something to save for next year and keep him
looking forward.

It isn't big.

There's the Sky Tower. They are asking an outrageous
amount to go up a steel spike inside its circular viewing
cabin so that you can look down on Rhyl. He had never done
that. It's shut. As is the Sun Centre and the Seaquarium.
According to the plaque he was probably not old enough
to remember the pier which is why he doesn't miss it now.

Sitting on the sea wall, the only comfortable position
is back to the sea though, he eats whiting and chips out
of a tray and takes a phone call. A husky-voiced woman
from Orange tells him he has no credit left – a variation of
what he's been hearing from Josie lately and he feels a silly,
uncomplicated pleasure at the cleverness of his own his
wisecrack. But it soon dissipates. Thanks Josie.

Something else he has never done: he abandons the

unfinished food and its packaging and walks off, getting lower and lower in the process, not bothering where he's heading. He knocks into somebody but nothing occurs.

Either he can drink which means he is here overnight – another expense unless he sleeps in the car for a few hours or – or what? He pauses to watch the waves roll in, driving back the dog walkers. Folding chairs are being snapped shut as the flasks go into carrier bags. This close the water is dishwater and never was the blue you could scoop up by the handful . . . A couple near him tuck into Rhyl Specials (hot dogs garnished with fried egg, a new delicacy) and you can tell the husband – a short bald fatty but better off than his wife in a wheelchair – you can tell he'd like to say something. Eryl blanks him and moves. From below a baby is set off for no apparent cause, its rising regular shriek louder than a car alarm.

To walk out on your own children and Josie – he argues with himself but the threads disintegrate. Being here as a kid. The holiday spirit. If the town's turned to shit on you. What d'you deserve? Like Josie said. You was always nothing you. Not as if you've got much to live up to. Your own sister. Means well, yeah right. A parade of. What comes around – no that wasn't it. Slapper she is. I'm stopping' them going there from now –

And then he sees it. Above beach level and facing inland: in common with most of Rhyl's newer constructions, the purpose isn't immediately obvious. Steps lead up to one long grey curve of wall with bits of colour applied . . . is how it looks at first. And second.

War Memorial? No one else is near and he wanders

closer across sand piled into mini dunes and crunchy with litter. It is a memorial. To a dead town. The inside surface of wall (cut with squares and rectangles of differing sizes but rebated) houses pictures that are tiles, photographs of Rhyl made into tiles. Well put-on tiles he notes, professionally speaking. With what's left of a fingernail he tries the glaze of one, then another. No lizard tails, smooth and invulnerable even though what's being celebrated is in landfill – or the crematorium. Cafes and ice cream carts and men in caps with their vintage cars and paddling pools and three wheeler bicycles and domes on buildings and fancy railings – and the crowds filling up the spaces in between are all long gone. But that stout woman in the tight trousers with her Jack Russell posed in front of the clock – Woolworths occupies the rest of the background – she is permanent. Eryl bets she wishes she had held her belly in.

MOMENTS IN TIME is carved along the top. He almost gets it. The wall is big and curved and the tiles are small in comparison and – but no. That's it. Yet he can't help but look at the donkeys, the smilers and wavers and guzzlers, the swimmers, the sunbathers so thickly packed they cover the sand and the pictures that are so old they are monochrome and the people in fancy dress, gurning mourners. The Pier has been caught before they knocked it down. Now he knows what was denied him –

And there on one of the tiles is him.

He is a supporting act, the snap having been of something else: the monorail that ran along the Front for a single season – why? – and which he'd forgotten till this instant. The holidaymakers are none too impressed by the way they're passing underneath it or lazing around not bothering to look up. It runs over their heads but they are too busy walking and laughing and counting their change. They are an unbuttoned-collars-and-black-bra-straps-showing sort of crowd, not a straw hat nor tube of sunblock between them. And just there, a part of it all but looking straight into the camera is himself. Lanky already in long trousers and a Wrexham FC home strip top, no sign of his mother or Uncle Pete, the hair's in his eyes and the expression on his face says –

It is him.

He tries staring out young Eryl. Cocky? Had he labelled the digger driver cocky? It was nothing by comparison to – free of grown-ups and with the run of whole Sunny Rhyl – his lead-guitarist stare. It is wounding to see. The sensation is of a sliver of rock, stuck half-way. You can't get it back up and you can't face the pain of swallowing it down. You don't want to choke yet to cough is murder.

A cigarette would be perfect now – he actually pats his jacket pocket and experiences bereavement. Consider the others, then: an old stallholder with bad teeth offers buckets and spades. 'Perv written all over.' A light aircraft lands on the beach though a crash is what the onlookers are wanting. The Marine Lake's so packed with boats you can hardly see lake – a child overboard would never be recovered. A pretty young blonde in a blue dress proudly displays her newborn in a pram, its father beside her already bored, disengaged . . . By counting this many up and this many across, he'll be able to explain how to find him again – how to pinpoint Eryl. (Who would that be to?

Who would want the information?) I'm ten or eleven, he is saying, and by the looks of it, Junior Eryl is having a blinding time. Before we'd dropped in on Queen Fatima.

By five o'clock the place has a packed-up air with a stream of traffic on the road towards the bridge and on to Abergele. People must actually work in Rhyl, a final surprise. It would be the easiest thing to stop off in one of the side-streets and heave a slab of Carling onto the passenger seat, take all the ifs and buts out of where he will sleep tonight. A quick Barclays Bank if he has the energy. A waking by seagull alarm.

With the car recovered and the heat evacuated, he cruises back along the Prom, 'Why does it always rain on me?' blasting out the Neptune Bar. A drive by the Eryl Bennion Shrine seems a must if only to pay respect. He considers getting out but the first gobbets of rain hit the windscreen. Of course. When he breaks off – he has been carrying the song on – it's to heckle the singer and still out loud. 'Thanks Travis! Lightning next, is it?'

... if this was the DVD they'd pump up the volume then lose it again in the downpour. If I was directing I'd leave present day Eryl right here right now soaked to the skin and standing guard on the Eryl Bennion tile. Like he'd died. Or you could make a proper film about the few of us up there. Keep it tight. Most of them being passed on by now, Eryl could play up-front. He could be somebody on that sort of team. Survivors Athletic – hit them with my story about visiting Queen Fatima and how it's been since then.

The scripting of it gets him along the Front, a right turn

comes up before he can anticipate a decision, which is made by the car. And the sea has vanished from the mirror when he checks next.

... Queen Fatima! She was wearing a gold bikini top. Sauce had dribbled down the front. Old as my gran she was – It wouldn't be a proper film you'd go out to see but one of the boring ones they put on late night when they know we're all too pissed to bother.

They're cheap to make Josie had said when he complained once. They've not got any actors in – just people.

# A CRACK

She sat up so abruptly her head bounced once, twice against the panelling that clothed the gable-end wall. That double bump had Saul instantly alert. The violence of the impact should have been enough to rouse a drunk. But she seemed perversely attached to her dream. Though the eyes were open and staring they were set in a sleeper's mask of paralysis. Only the pulling back and down of the corners of her mouth signalled to Saul that any moment now, Julianne would wake. But there was still a phase that had to be got through. He saw the huge gulp of breath causing her chest to swell, the dark nipples leaping on the white skin.

She screamed.

Gathered in more breath.

Screamed again.

No actor asked for agony could have been more convincing. When first he'd heard it his own sympathetic system had adrenalized him too. (Crazy with fear, is how he'd described it to Julianne later, when she'd asked, seeming cool and curious that first time). Now, as she was about to repeat the process, he took her by one shoulder not caring whether his nails cut into it. 'Jules. *Julianne*! It's all right. You're dreaming. Jules, wake up!'

As always happened – as always failed to happen – she didn't turn to him. Instead she sank back against the wall, bumping her head one last time while her naked upper torso collapsed into the pillows. Hands that seemed alien to her came up to rub the tightened cheeks. Splayed fingers ran through moist hair and then back to her forehead. Even in this half-light Saul could see how panic had made a stranger of her. She was a fine-boned, prettyish, terrified woman that he'd never seen before – nor cared about. For a moment, at least.

'Jules. OK? You awake?'

A pointless enquiry. If she weren't, the ear-splitting racket would still be going on. It would be rebounding off that high beam at the room's apex. It would be seeping through the inadequate party-wall on the other side of which old Mrs Bellinger had just been catapulted back into consciousness.

Saul leaned across to the bedside table and grasped the plastic mug of water (Jules had broken two tumblers) and drank greedily. 'There's some left. D'you want a drink?'

'Um. Yes. If you've got some there.'

'I have. I said so.'

He passed the cup and she clawed for it.

'Thanks.'

'OK now?'

'I'm – Yes, I'm out of it.'

Interesting. She'd not used that phrase before. Interesting.

'Was it the same? Same dream? You were screaming again – 'nough to wake the dead.'

'What? No. It's not the same . . . never the same. I'm sorry. Sorry.'

'That's all right.'

'Sorry, anyway.'

'It's not as if you can help it,' he conceded.

'No. Well.'

They half-lay, half-sat, in parallel and untouching. His nostrils filled with the floral scent of her shampoo raised in sweat. There was his own salt-maleness also. 'I'll go and make tea,' he offered.

'No. No I think –' she slipped downwards and hunched away still further, 'I'll give it another go. What is it now? It feels early – 'bout five?'

He groped amongst assorted objects on his own side. 'Ten to.'

'Fuck.'

Just as he was drifting off again he felt her shift abruptly. When he opened his eyes he found he was staring straight into hers – but she was looking past him, looking over his shoulder at something that had become more visible in the few minutes the light had had to strengthen. 'The door,' she said. 'It's closed. I like it open a crack.'

Saul rolled smoothly out from beneath the covers and into the cool air, as though by practise. The lock complained and three floors of the flimsy building shuddered as he yanked at the handle. But in the morning the door was shut.

Beyond their garden of wet paving Culham's village green had been recently doused. Each blade of grass was tipped with a brilliant point – and looking up Saul found bushes and trees (even those still sunk in dormancy) all zinging with reflective energy. He avoided the turf to preserve his shoes; it had the added advantage of giving Mrs Bellinger and mongrel Lotty the slip. The dog was over-sociable and would try to decorate his chinos with its prints but that mattered less than having to own up to hoping *they hadn't disturbed her again last night.* He hurried forward, a sudden interest in the sign of The Lion pub keeping his gaze safely above her head. At the very edge of vision he saw Lotty perform an effortless vault into the graveyard surrounding St Paul's church, Mrs Bellinger's pleas doing nothing to slow its progress over sacred ground. It had been the latest Spring he could remember since first coming to Oxford as a student more than a decade ago, but the daffodils were finally out. Lotty was trashing them.

The air though delicious was frigid for April but still a few hardy bees were up, working blossom that peppered the blackthorn hedges. Everywhere it seemed life was making its bid. His bus stop stood opposite the small Culham Parochial Primary School. Already the playground was being crossed and re-crossed by a band of children. Vibrant reds in their clothing overwhelmed the strip of washed lawn and surrounding trees. They reminded Saul that his own daughter would be setting out for nursery school about this time. Padded against the chill, but tiny, in her red shoes, minute buckled shoes like a doll's, face sparkling with tears – surely a false image? She'd be strapped into the back seat of Kate's car, chattering the drive away through the Cardiff suburbs. Why, in the name of all of the Gods, couldn't his ex-wife have just –? But then why couldn't he have just –? It was an uncomfortable line of thought and one he needed to snap. Work, new work, that was the ticket. And when Virgil was your man, what better for a Spring day than . . . *Just get to it,* he told himself. (The bus came into view). *Protinus aerii mellis caelestria.* Grinning he rendered it as *get going with that heaven-sent-honey-thing, dude . . . Now!*

Aristaeus, Virgil's beekeeper from *The Georgics,* duly obliged this morning though he took the form of a headache. Saul found the myth of Aristaeus had boarded the bus with him and now offered itself up in throbbing hexameters. The story was simple enough. Aristaeus, the first ever beekeeper, had lost his bees as punishment from Mount Olympus – for sexual indiscretion, what else? Had lost face presumably by having lost his bees. Yet the myth concerned itself mainly with grief and despair . . . and whining. A lot of whining from bad-boy Aristaeus. He runs after the wrong woman, is thwarted and caught out, and it's *Oh mother, my care and skill have availed me naught – and you, my mother have not warded off from me the blow of this misfortune.* Cyrene, the mother, the water-nymph . . .

The bus crossed the broad, sluggish Culham Cut and then the unruly Thames itself, leaving Culham village by the roundabout route – because, just like Aristaeus, Saul had lost something. He had lost sleep, had failed to recapture sleep after Julianne's nightmare drove it off, had dozed stupidly around seven and never caught up with a routine that should have ended with a successful boarding of the direct bus into the city.

*Sleep was like a bee-swarm . . . curling darkly through*

*the field of vision, never settling, never stilled . . . and then as the buzzing – more a droning really, a sustained droning . . . though a falling one, down and down another octave until . . .*

A scratchy blow delivered to the side of his face by a woman's shopping basket restored him to life as a bus passenger. He turned to eye-curse her uncaring back. Tweed coat with a smattering of light animal hair, thick legs in sensible boots, the ancient basket, the paperback emerging the instant she sat: the woman had professor's wife written through her like seaside rock.

'Oh, hello Dr Prothero!' Someone was addressing him. Someone was pronouncing his name Prother-oo, taking away the Welsh tinge and elongating it to joke-Scottiness, 'Didn't notice you there.' The woman's face became one he knew. It became Maggie's, a 'scout' in his own workplace, Jesus College. *Jesus College, Maggie! HQ of the Oxford University Welsh – so what's so hard about Prothero, eh? Eh, Maggie?*

The bus lurched on. The drumming settled to a hum in his temples.

Where, even once safely static at his desk, it persisted. Still the beekeeper maintained his tenancy of Saul's head. *Care and skills have availed me naught* – what was implied? That knowledge itself is a fickle deity? Don't feel too smug if you've been accepted into that particular cult. The epic's grid of tensions was offering him something new here. The bees, then – *yes,* the bees became peripheral. Learning, *Scientia* even, is suspect, a tawdry wizardry that leaves the business of life, of real human life, side-lined. But –

Below him in Second Quad, a girl's train of sorrel hair

snaffled his attention. She was an unknown, a visitor for a meritless student – perhaps one of his own – who was idling the morning away in a plush cell. As she floated across the face of the golden wall opposite latent wisteria, tortured and pinioned there, stirred in sympathy. Young tendrils yearned though the horny grey snakes of its branches played dead. *Vivamus mea Lesbia, atque amemus.* The same breeze that had set the daffodils jittering now snatched hold of the girl's light skirt, displaying her outline in stirring clarity, hips, pubic bone, long slim thighs . . . between Jules and himself nothing was happening. Her work had always both fulfilled and exhausted and these sleep problems . . . or psychological problems – there he had admitted it to himself, there was some mental thing going on . . . he didn't know what. How could he be expected to know what? This mental thing was whisking her away to a private underworld, its fumes polluting daytime. He tried to recall when sex had last seemed like a possibility. Not when it had actually taken place but when the frisson of it had spiced up a Sunday lie-in or a rainy afternoon, a hint of chilli on the tongue. Failed. She of the glowing hair passed over the grass leaving no print and disappeared into the dark passage that led to Third Quad. Deeper into the college: the gate into Ship Street being locked as a security measure, she'd need to pass beneath his window, would need to display herself to him again if she were ever to get out. Life in college had its attractions. Perhaps during the week it would make more sense . . . ?

As displacement activity, he Googled beekeeping, only cancelling the search when Maggie put her head around the door. She was returning a waste paper basket he hadn't missed. 'Thanks Maggie.' When she'd gone he typed in Night + terrors. Yawned. Waited, finding that sustained note accompanying the yawning process hung on well after the yawn was complete.

'Today's had a theme to it,' he told Julianne as they prepared for bed. 'Well, a theme and a sub-theme, to be completely accurate.' He paused for any encouraging signal. She was bending down, placing the belt she'd just detached from a pair of trousers into the lowest drawer. Her bra was a white strip across her narrow back, her panties a pair of white lace shorts, pulled tight across a dark cleft. 'There was a sort of basket-thing going on – from bee-skeps, I think. Had this idea about the Aristaeus myth from *The Georgics* – the science of beekeeping. On the bus.' Even as she was straightening up he saw her shoulders hunch. He tried to forestall mockery. 'Yeah, yeah, *I know.*'

Each vertebra was too well defined, her complete spine sharp as a row of teeth. He walked over, pulled her to him and slipped his hands around her waist, cupping the floating ribs, down across her concave belly.

'I'm really wrecked,' she said.

'Yes, you must be. I'm –'

'Latham now claims to have found a flaw in the initial protocol.'

'Uh-huh?'

'The original license was for toxicity-testing. By adding environmental factors – my idea, as you know, I added close confinement of each subject animal, then noise stress, finally the –'

'I get it.'

'He says to hold off until he's reviewed the entire series.'

'Ah.'

'It was my protocol,' she said, pushing off with enough force to make him step back. *The whole series.* Half a million in costs. Two hundred experimental animals in total. And that's not counting all the –' All the not-worth-counting-things the gesture finished. 'Did I say? I've got to get in early tomorrow?'


Dawn had found numerous small entries into their bedroom, sufficient for him to see her eyes' glitter. They were focused on nothing. But whatever they saw was causing her to shriek . . . to sob. This time there was something pleading in each drawn-out finale, each hopeless gasp by lungs emptied and raw.

'Jules! Wake up.'

The arm he had a hold of was slick and she caught him across the bridge of the nose as she fought to pull free. *Ohgodohgodohgodohgod* – the incantation came up to the threshold of comprehension. But she was easily subdued. For an instant he visioned himself weighty and powerful, forcing a woman down into the bed. As she fell back panting he had to throw himself sideways to keep from crushing her. His hand slipped across her breasts and their alert nipples as he let go. But there was nothing to be felt on that score. Hardly awake himself yet he was depressingly aware of this absence at least. No jolt, no swell of feeling . . . no swell.

In silence he drank from the plastic mug with its plastic-tainted water, passed it back. 'Drink up, I'll refill it.' If she drank it all he could get fresh, drink fresh himself and wash away the taste. 'Look I'll – just sit there a minute. I'll be back in a minute. I want to say something.'

She was upright when he returned and for an instant he was tempted to slide over. But the gathering light showed the set of her features, the way the cheek bones formed a perfectly aligned counterpoint to arched brows. His heart hardened. A flaw, a lack of symmetry, something to forgive and cherish was what he needed. Was absent. 'We can't have this just going on and on – it's been weeks. You have to try and explain to me what's happening.'

'Can't.'

'What are they about? The dreams.'

'I've told you they're not dreams.'

'Nightmares, then.'

'They're not nightmares.'

License had been given now for anger. But he reminded himself he'd been angry with her before the questioning and lack of satisfactory response. He acted gentleness. 'All right. You tell me if you can, what is happening when you wake up like this. What is it that's making you so scared?"

She nodded. But, 'I can't tell you,' she said.

'Why not?'

'Because –' if a lie were on its way now she didn't flinch from looking at him as she said it, 'I'm not able. I think I said it before. I just . . . can't . . . say.'

'But you know?'

'Please Saul.'

'Please what? I'm trying to help.'

'But it won't help. I can't do what – I can't do.'

'Is it always the same?' He hoped to catch her off-guard, the way a student's shallow take on his topic could be exposed by a casual observation, something tangential, an innocent remark the poor undergraduate brain lacked the nous to leave alone.

'Sort of.'

'A *similar* story then, if not always the same one?'

'There's no story.'

It was time to take her in his arms. Saul let his hand burrow out a passage between her burning back and the hot pillow and found how easily she flicked across – how much weight had she lost in these last few weeks? – and settled against him. 'There's gotta be a story, sweetness. Everything's got a story. Dreams are the stories we tell ourselves. And we tell stories because –'

'Well there isn't. There's this –' she considered for a long while . . . a very long while. The house, a two centuries old structure creaked and settled above their heads. Beyond it, the village was so still Saul could hear his own blood's regular progression around his body, through the neck, across the eardrums and back to source. Impossible to ignore once noticed. And then all the wait preluded was, 'There's this feeling. Awful. No – beyond awful. There . . . aren't . . . words.' Through their joint heat, she shivered. 'No bloody words. I've got no words.'

'But you're feeling things.'

'Yes.'

'Fear?' Curiosity at least could become aroused – with the remembered force of lust.

'Yes. Well, I don't know. *That's it.* There are . . . terrible things. I can feel a terrible thing. But no words – I haven't any. I'm me. While it's happening, I *think* I know I'm me. I know that it's me it's happening to, at any rate. But I don't have a word, not even for myself.'

'So is that what's so frightening? You do seem *really scared* while you're, you know, shouting out.'

'No.' He felt her chest heave. 'No, there's something going on. Some . . . things are going on. I'm frightened of these things that happen to me. It's worse than you can imagine. I never knew you could feel such –'

'Such what?'

'I don't know.'

She turned on her side, shoved her head roughly beneath his chin and started to cry. He felt the stickiness of tears as the sobs grew in intensity. Saliva, he registered now, dribbling as her open mouth tried to drag in sufficient oxygen . . . and now came snot, oozing from her pressed-out-of-shape nose.

'*Come on.* It can't be that bad. Come on. We'll get through it. It'll stop, you'll see. These things come and go, huh?'

He stroked the short, springy hair back from her ears and felt the skull beneath. He was willing a response, willing her to meet him half-way as he thought of it, to admit that what was going on was unusual, a blip – or series of blips at least. That soon they'd reclaim the life they'd shared a few months ago, content, unencumbered, collusive in a limited range of pleasures.

'Why can't that bloody door stay open?' she mumbled. 'I like the door open.'

Although it was his turn to take the car, he gave it up. Julianne's work lay to the south behind wire fencing and threatening signage, a mere fifteen minutes drive. Bus routes North into the city were more numerous, though the journeys longer. But something in her expression had made him hand over the keys, to offer a small easement – anything to slacken off the worry lines. Behind her eyes lurked an atavistic wariness this morning. He'd tried to put a hand out as she swept up her stuff with the briefest of acknowledgements but, tired himself, had mistimed it, fumbled the opportunity behind her back, all his reflexes shot to crap.

So the bus for him, again . . . and there was more to this Aristaeus bloke than he'd first thought. According to Virgil the bees, the lost bees, were recovered only following a plot complex and comical as light opera. Inevitably, sacrifice is what's needed – on Aristaeus' part. The valuable beasts (cattle) are sacrificed, the bees consent to return and build in their carcases. *Yuk*, he thought. The bacon roll resurfacing like oleum added its garnish to a general malaise and a specific throb in the sinuses. Weary, that was all. Once it would hardly have registered. Lack of sleep playing hell with his chemistry which Julianne could explain, no doubt. Well into his thirties, he was bound to be nurturing those physical tics and weaknesses that were going to make the downhill years increasingly –

*What was up, now? Get a grip! Get back to it!*

Aristaeus was forced to appeal to the Gods – wasn't that the ancient moral? Beyond the understanding of the pathetic apiarist (still running home to Mummy, please note, when his bees go and defect) he's saved by traditional wisdom wrapped up in religiosity. Everywhere the major themes of the Ancients resurface: Don't get above yourself. Defer to the past. Don't break the rules. *You will pay for it.*

Jules had been working on her current project for two and a half years. They'd been together for about that – up and down. *The environmental stressors . . . as you know, my idea.* Why had the visitations been delayed, if here was their inspiration? If that's where these nocturnal horrors sprang from? Because what she did, of course, would be enough to give most people the creeps. He'd never say this to her, naturally. What she did was, if not an ethical problem, then . . . and it might be – yes, it might be, he wasn't sure, wasn't going to think let himself think about it for long enough to ever get near to being *sure*. If not an ethical problem, then, an aesthetic one. At the very least it was that. The shining clarity of the cornea corroded beneath the drops . . . or the shaven skin peeled away to the body's living pulp . . . He could never catch sight of her neat, thin hands – red with scrubbing, itchy from that hibi-scrub sensitivity she was managing – and not feel, well, he had to say it now and, though he was alone amongst strangers on a bus, though he was talking to himself in the privacy of his own brain and still it was only just safe to say it.

What Jules did freaked him out.

*What Jules did* ... no, no, *no!* ... what Aristaeus did, what he was instructed to do, was sacrifice. Four bulls and four cows 'of equal beauty'. Yeah, right, you could imagine that. *The Task.* Some task. Cattle were so big and bony, with their square frames bursting through skins hung on them like canvas ... draping itself into hollows behind the ribs, as though some big important organs had been whipped out ... *what Jules did* –

'Maggie!' his mouth greeted her of its own accord. 'I never knew you lived over this way.'

'Just the thirty-odd years,' she said without rancour.

Maggie looked older, close-to. The roots of her brass-coloured hair were silvery and her jawline a vague boundary between face and neck. 'My partner –' he said, 'she works down on the Reading road, at the – at a lab. So we live half-way between –'

'That'll be the one where there's been all that trouble?' she offered. Ever helpful, that was Maggie.

'Yes.'

'If this big one, this big new lab, comes to Oxford – you know they're going to use the monkeys in it, they say? There's going to be ructions. That's what they're saying. I mean they've had the police to your wife's place again this week. It was on the radio – one of the protestors is in the John Radcliffe. Fractured skull. And with this new one it'll be ten times worse. So they say. Your wife's place'll be nothing –'

'We're not married, actually. But it's not that simple, the animal question, is it? Obviously people feel strongly both ways. I'm a classicist, of course, so I can't pretend to be in on the science but Julianne, that's my partner, she –'

'Oh, sorry, Dr Protheroo. There's my friend just got on. We sit together.'

He turned away to find they were passing the well-tended entrance to Radley ; it was the school he'd fantasized his daughter might one day attend. When she was old enough. When they admitted girls or perhaps they did now. In another moment the road ran between fields again, an opportunity for trying to spot *beautiful cows*.


Friday. These days they could put off anything like conversation till a Friday evening. Home before Jules – he defoliated parsley stalks and dismembered vegetables on a wooden board with no clear idea of the dish that needed these ingredients. Beyond the kitchen window and their own straggling shrubs, Mrs Bellinger had dug a trench the size of a child's grave. Now she was forking in the contents of the huge heap of rotted stuff beside it. Every one of the cottages in the row contributed to the thing. The sweet peppers' innards, woody mushroom stalks, and onion skins littering the worktops would be added soon. Mrs Bellinger's heap – there was an element of compulsion about the thing. *I was born in this house. Four of us, there was. My old dad grew enough on this one plot to feed us all. And my brothers were big eaters! When we were kiddies we'd bring the grass from off the green by the barrow-load. My dad mowed it for nothing just for the clippings. Gets the compost going like nothing else. Just feel that heat come off when you walk past!* Steam was rising from each forkful. Vigilant Mrs Bellinger examined every deposit, occasionally diving in with bare, stained hands to extract a fragment of yoghurt pot or an indigestible foil top. Lotty was in continual trouble for interference – in fact, Saul decided, the two were a neat tableau of mutual incomprehension. The old woman labouring at a task that surely could have no pleasure in it and no real point, the animal's mistaking items of poly- propylene or tin as significant rather than the trash they were . . .

'Hi.'

Jules had arrived in the kitchen, her coat already off, her case abandoned somewhere. She was all in black, black trousers, black sweater, black boots. Her pink scarf was in her hands, being wrapped around her hands, rolled and twisted, tested: well up to the strain being put on it, though, like gristle.

'Hello. Didn't hear you there. Next door's dog –'

'It's happened! The whole thing. What I said about Latham? We've had a meeting today.' She came and sank onto the stool near to where he was engaged, her look straight out of the window but not taking in the old woman and dog. Apparently. 'He's going to bury the lot.'

'Oh-h. *Infesta hostilis exercitus itinera,*' he said recklessly quoting Tacitus. Julianne stared. 'Threatening movements by the enemy on land.' For reckless read *insane*, he thought. Too late. 'I'm – sorry. Very sorry.'

Obviously what must be done was abandon the food- thing. Pour some wine, take her into the room which they called the sitting room though they hardly ever sat in it. The next time they locked glances, her eyes were suffused with redness and then overflowing. But they fell into chairs across from each other, either side of the empty fireplace. Now he must lean over to pat her knee. 'Don't cry, Jules. I know it's easy for me to say. But – look . . . whatever you've had going on – at work I mean, it's been doing bad deeds to your head, love. These nightmares . . . call them what you like, you can't pretend it hasn't been crap – You're thrashed most of the time.' *We both are,* he knew he mustn't add. 'Maybe it's for the best for things to come to out in the open like this. Maybe you've been worried about its not going well. Maybe that's what's been nagging at you and now –'

'*What?* I don't know what you're talking about.' Half of the Waitrose' best went down her throat in a single gulp, unnoticed. A bloody droplet fell onto her trousered thigh and disappeared. She knocked back the remainder. 'There was never any question of me being worried about work – or not until Latham got involved, I wasn't. *Extra* involved. He holds the license. That's what he reminded us of this afternoon. At the meeting. *I hold the license for all animal experimentation in the whole of this facility. Including this series. Let nobody forget that. It's my name, my reputation.* Can you believe it?' Saul could think of no reason why not to believe it but she ploughed on anyway. 'Why would I be worried about work, huh? Until this week *work* has been really good. Better than good. It was *going great.*'

Chopping hands added to the intensity of what was meant to be a put-down exit. She jumped to her feet. 'I'm going to get changed.'

'No – just hang on. Stay and talk. Just –' Why wouldn't she sit again? He was being forced to lean back, to look up but at least she lingered. 'I'm . . . not so hot myself, as it happens. I – I find myself thinking about Lowri. ' Lowri was his daughter. 'A lot. More than a lot. Really missing her. I need to go and see her more often. And to see Cate, actually.' Cate, as in Lowri's mother: Jules had met neither, knew them only as names – but what names! Spoken aloud, embedded in these sentiments, they must sound heavy as Yahweh.

He had downed his own wine too quickly in an effort to match her. Certainly the glass, when he noticed it, was empty – and on standing, he found the entire room twitch across his field of vision. And his head buzzed. But if Jules had understood all that he intended her to understand, she chose not to react. He fell back on trying to imagine how she must feel. Here he was, in her face, close enough to touch but not touching. Instead he was saying words that couldn't be taken back. He was hearing them for the first time, himself, so he knew they were powerful. Powerful things, words, in any language you liked. 'I'm thinking of going up to Cardiff,' he said. 'Tomorrow, probably. For the day – or two.'

'Are you?'

'So if there's anything I can do – before I go . . . ?'

The house became very quiet. But then it was a quiet little place, Culham, in comparison to the city, which is why they'd chosen it, with a quiet lane running through it, and they had such quiet neighbours. Even that buzzing in his head had stopped . . . yes, definitely stopped.

And Jules, she'd taken all this quietly, the mental trouble, whatever that was all about (he supposed he'd never know) and the crisis at work and now this – *this* pronouncement that he'd sprung on them both. She seemed to be taking it pretty calmly. She was picking up her bag and briefcase, throwing her black coat over her arm in preparation for its transference to their shared wardrobe. The stairs wound up from the room they were in; Julianne halted at the bottom as though about to speak – just as a last glimmer of sun thrust in, low enough to drive a bright tunnel through the house, catching her before she stepped into shadow, leaving her dazzled and vulnerable. And all he could think was how this mourning black was doing her no good, how it turned her skin to grey-taupe.

Whatever it was she intended didn't get said. Lotty's high-pitched *yip* came next, sudden as a weapon's report. And when she opened her mouth a second time, *Yip-yip-yip-yip!* Lotty countered.

'Jules?'

'You can do something for me, actually,' she said. 'Before you go. That old woman from next door? Tell her from me, will you, to *get that dog of hers to shut the fuck up?*'

# THAT STORY

. . . and the saddest thing – she corrected herself, *one* of the saddest things being that the child was so very beautiful. A little girl of nearly six months, she wore her father's black hair as a neat cap marking out a high forehead and delicate widow's peak. But it was the eyes that snatched at you, huge, luminous eyes with already a spark of joyful intelligence. They were fixed on Glenda's face now and a set of miniature fingers reached out toward it.

Glenda Powell had to swallow hard before saying, 'The point is Ashley, she'll be sitting up any day now, won't she?'

Unlike Baby Naila, Ashley would look anywhere but directly at her. 'I don-n think so,' she mumbled. 'Seven months they said – down the clinic.'

'For some babies it can be as young as five.'

'My mam said seven.'

'*Anyway*, it'll be soon. So what we need to talk about is how you can look after Naila when she does.'

Ashley Foulkes let out a theatrical sigh making the baby blink at being blown on. Ashley was a bulky nineteen-year-old and her naked upper arm was well capable of obscuring the child which it did now. Glenda had to shift to keep Naila in view. 'She'll be all right. My mam says –'

'So long as you remember a baby of this age will try to sit up and then topple over. So if she's not in a safe place and well padded around – just think.'

'I'm not bloody stupid.' Ashley adjusted a bright red strap in danger of burying itself in her flesh, then followed the movement through by plunging a hand down below the T-shirt neckline and rummaging around, settling breasts that must be uncomfortable. 'Not gonna sit her on the worktop am I – and then go and sod off?' She turned to look at the child for the first time as though expecting her to show some support. Obligingly Naila chuckled.

Glenda said, 'Could we have Baby out please, for a minute?'

'She's only just gone down. Tired.'

'Only for a minute.'

'Come 'ere then.' Ashley plucked up the small body. At the moment of suspension the feet of the baby-grow hung well below Naila's actual little feet. The buggy was parked in the centre of the room, parallel to the sofa Ashley was on – and furthest off from Glenda's chair. But instead of coming closer, she leaned back and away, clutching Naila to her chest and letting a heap of magazines topple onto the rug. Over the sofa arm she seemed to become interested in the cover of *Heat*: a long thin celebrity in a swimsuit was draped across a sunlounger, every tooth revealed, champagne flute raised. Glenda might as well not have been there.

Apart from sofa and chair, the room had no other furniture. A television was attached to one wall, a frameless mirror to another. But since Glenda's last visit, each corner had been filled up with a mixture of new goods still in their cartons, untidily stacked and some opened. Plenty of disposable nappies were a rational acquisition and to be encouraged, but there were also cardboard boxes of tinned food, catering packs of sugar sachets and eye-bath-sized milks. Yet more glossies were sealed in plastic envelopes. The magazines came from a grandfather who worked for a recycling firm, Glenda had been told – *so like I'm not buying them*. The rest was a new phenomenon – though even these were capable of positive interpretation. Glenda visited clients where there was no food of any kind, ever, either on show or in store. They were always *going down the shops . . .*

Ashley seemed to have fallen into a daze in the heat of the late summer afternoon. Glenda could just about reach the baby and run one hand over Naila's velvet crown to the back of her head, saying as she did so, 'Hello Naila, how are you today?' Naila shrieked with pleasure. 'This spot we talked about on her scalp – here it is, yes? It feels worse today if anything.'

'Grows that way.'

'*No.* Your health visitor, Marie Raglan – she explained. If you leave Baby too long on her back, if you don't pick her up and talk to her, play a little game – come on Ashley you know all this.' But for the smile to be accepted it needed Ashley to look at her. 'Naila gets bored. She *wants* to use her brain. You might have a genius on your hands, eh? So the head rocking is something she can do to pass the time and try to cheer herself up. That's why the skin is tender here – where I'm showing you now.' She dare not touch the angry blemish. 'Her hair's worn away. She *has* to be got out of her buggy –'

'I do.'

'No. Because the hair would be growing back if Naila was on your knee more often or in the carrier going around the house with you . . . seeing things as you moved.'

'What's there to see?' In her next breath the subject lurched towards the familiar one, namely, the unfairness of Masood, the baby's father, *being sent back.* She elaborated on the difficulties this was causing her, giving her depression and Naila *was picking it up and getting upset as well.*

'But having Naila with you and paying her more attention might help. She's a beautiful little girl. I'll bet when you take her out other people tell you that. That must be nice to hear. You must be proud of her.'

'Yeah, well.'

'Why don't we give it a fortnight? And during that time could you, say, have Baby out of the buggy and in either the sling or the backpack while you're doing things in the house? Could you try that?'

'*Yes.*'

It didn't sound affirmative. But, 'Good,' Glenda said. 'I'll pop in again. If you can just – look, she's really coming on. She'll be sitting up soon, as I said. You can take her from room to room then so long as you pad her well.' Ashley slid Naila down onto a Mickey Mouse cover being used as an under-blanket. Over-heating in this weather and not too clean – *one thing at a time,* though. 'Ring if you need a chat. You have my number. Yes?' Then breaking her own rule she said, 'Isn't it hot today? I'd let her cool off a little now. No need to wrap her up if you've got her on a quilt. '

In the dim hall corridor, she and Ashley were squeezed together. The smell of Ashley's under-arm, sickly sweet and chemical, came wafting up as she fumbled with the lock. Frustration got the better of Glenda: 'They're babies for such a short time.' She stepped out and turned. 'You'll be glad you enjoyed her as much as you could!' She was about to embark on an incident from her own daughter's first year but Ashley had shut the door. Glenda was alone on the half landing with the echoing footsteps of other tenants hurrying down and then a double bang and the rush of air which told of escape. Shouldering her bag, she followed them out to Butetown's sweltering rim.

The day had turned sultry with fumes drifting and set-tling between the rows and blocks that stood less than half a mile from Cardiff Bay and open sea – though you would never know it. Once the poor clustered at the water's edge, now they were being pushed back from it. For a moment she lingered unable to prevent herself looking up at the first floor of the low-rise that was Letton House – from which Ashley Foulkes stared down. Of Naila there was no sign: back in her buggy, of course. Now Ashley drew one curtain. Glenda visualised the scene as the reflections off the TV and mirror that had attracted the child's eyes even with the flicker of a passing pigeon, were dimmed. Naila's head scanned left and right at a featureless ceiling, search-ing, waiting.

The car was unbearable. She had to open every window and then cringe from it, retreating to smoke her fifth cigarette of the day in the shade of a row of garages. This had the added advantage of shielding her completely from Letton, a building with its own story. Tom 'the Fish' Letton, a local street seller had been known for his kindness to friend and stranger alike. For nearly half a century, beginning sometime between the two world wars, he had given charity under the pretence of credit to families who would not otherwise have eaten. No reason that was ever discovered, no agenda. He had organised football for the area's roaming children and just gave away most of what came his way. But on Glenda's first visit, Jerry her team manager had read the plaque put up beyond the graffiti line, read it out loud and responded with a disbelieving, 'Good God!'

Jerry was at his desk still. Between deep inhalations Glenda reminded him where she had been and sketched in the Ashley situation: Baby, bright though developmentally thwarted, evidence of food being purchased, but Mum irritable. In fact, so distracted, only capable of 'problem-focused talk' and lacking in cooperation. Ashley Foulkes' first baby, also a girl, was now three years old, a Cared-for Child in foster pending adoption. She could hear Jerry tapping away, adding today's observations without any of his own. 'See ya tomorrow. No I won't I'm – I'm somewhere,' he said, 'Tarr-ah!' . . . It was ten to six now. Groups of teenagers were still straggling in the vague direction of home, articles of grey uniforms draped around them rather than being worn, customised in most cases beyond recognising. A Catholic school was somewhere in the neighbourhood, St Saviour's she thought, or St Salvator's. An all-girl gaggle overtook her en route to the car. They parted around

Glenda, a middle-aged woman in a crumpled dress, as if she were a piece of pavement furniture, leaving a reek of make-up and hair products – and tobacco. Odd how the heat never relieved you of the desire to light up even on days like this one, attaching a permanent snake of sweat around the waist. Last winter she earmarked the long-distant summer as a good time to quit. Now the evening's failures were presenting themselves as already inevitable.

By the direction the ambulance was aimed for, the accident must be on the Central Link. Everything backed up: half an hour to get the five miles out to Penarth, and it was sizzle all the way. No weak-willed glancing towards the marina – a flat in Clive Place was home since her divorce. Then she must park in front of next door's. Not a real problem. He was manager of a restaurant across on Mermaid Quay, he was sleek and youthful and commuted by racing bike over the barrage though she still didn't know him to speak to. That's what she should do, she thought for the hundredth time, get a bike, give up smoking, lose some weight. Once out of the car she sucked in breath from the direction of a beach she still couldn't see, being two streets back and tried stretching herself to someone taller, fitter, more toned. Indoors, before anything else, before putting down the bits and pieces grabbed at lunchtime or opening the French windows, she leaned against the kitchen sink and rang Marie Raglan. She was not only Ashley's health visitor but Glenda's best friend. Glenda had a strong need to describe the unsatisfactory interview, to explore with Marie's help her concerns. They had been gnawing at her since leaving Butetown, had egged her on to have cigarette after cigarette, aggressing all the while at other motorists. Marie's phone rang once and switched to voicemail meaning probably with a client. Glenda texted Call me!! and walked out into her garden.

After the city, the atmosphere here was cooler – almost clean. For most of the year this north-facing courtyard was not really much of an asset. If she had bought the 'garden flat' with a fantasy of parties, laughter and music at a neighbourly-responsible level – Marie and a few carefully chosen others wander through the glass doors, drinks in hand, a good bloody red not champagne – it hadn't happened. Still, on a day like today the yard came into its own. The cold of the metal bench was delicious to her bare legs and helped subdue, if not her unease, then some of the hostile feeling towards Ashley. There was worse than Ashley among her case load and tomorrow one of them might demonstrate that little Naila was lucky, was a lottery winner . . . After a while she was calm enough to go back inside and eat from the open fridge a wedge of Brie with three wrinkled tomatoes. Then squatting on the cool tiles and armed with a spoon she followed them down with a peach melba yoghurt and another; all the yoghurts were this flavour, her least favourite. Now they reminded her of Ashley Foulkes' stock of goods, piled in a corner as though for – what? Disaster? The cartons had been labelled by hand: Beans With Sausage. Curry Beans. Mexican Bean Chilli. Glenda tipped a brace of custard tarts from their pack onto a plate, boiled the kettle for a cup of instant and took a bottle of water instead with her to the living room and the open laptop.

The local news' lead item was of four people dying in a house fire in Port Talbot, a girl of eight the only survivor and she was 'said to be very poorly in hospital'. One of her disappeareds – children who had been allocated a social worker, provided with an initial assessment and then been removed from the known address – had turned up in Port Talbot recently. With an 'auntie.' A bad situation was likely to get worse unless Jerry could decide on requesting police action and the police were willing to act . . . there you go, lucky little Naila.

She had just opened her Narratives file when the phone rang and she snatched it up. 'Marie! Thank-Christ!'

'Hello Mum.' It was her daughter, Kathryn.

'Sorry love. My mind was elsewhere. Must be the weather. I'm going off in all this heat.'

Kathryn ignored the attempt at humour. 'London's worse.' The snappish tone said something was wrong.

For ten minutes Glenda listened to the latest instalment of the battle with *Dr Dread* in the Department of Social Sciences. Kathryn, having returned to her old college as a postgrad after marriage and motherhood, now hustled herself from Ealing maisonette to nursery school to a University department where she was being supervised by a man younger than herself. On the plus side she was sticking with her husband and he with her. Dermot was someone Glenda approved of rather than liked though he seemed a faithful partner and a loving father. *Rare as the unicorn,* Glenda had said to Marie. Her daughter's current grievance was nothing to do with family: it centred on the collection of stories Glenda had been about to open. The research paper, 'Motifs of Childhood and Youth in Urban Myths' had been entirely Kathryn's. Only using Glenda as an unpaid field worker to gather Cardiff material had made it possible. Kathryn herself trawled London's available subcultures, the ancillary workers at Dermot's hospital and Eastern Europeans at the nursery where she deposited the children. Now that it looked promising Dr Laurens Harrell was taking a sudden, too keen an interest.

'Apparently it's always been a collaboration! Did you know that, Mum? You've been working for him all this time.'

Glenda mustered some of the required indignation – then added perhaps it was the price often paid working with a Name? . . . though no, *no*, of course *not fair!* Other slights were revisited until Kathryn's anger spent itself as they became sillier, *pathetic really,* and more distant. Luckily hers was not an obsessive personality. She could laugh at Glenda's suggestion of the deflationary ploy of breast-feeding at the next faculty meeting and finally be diverted to her two boys. They were thriving, developing ahead of the expected rate, in fact only yesterday or it might have been the day before . . . Glenda found herself responding mechanically to the voice at the other end. Lack of love for her grandsons wasn't responsible – in fact, an underlying general afraidness for them was ever present in her chest like inhaled dust. Toxic London, people's craziness, sickness, Dermot's medically-trained arrogance blinding him to the one symptom that must be caught in time. But Naila Foulkes' brilliant eyes were trying to fix on anything that moved – and then on Glenda, watching and pining for something to happen. Willing it to happen. Almost she broke in and told Kathryn, in general terms, about her anxieties for the little girl.

'. . . and Dermot said he'd take them both again next Saturday because they were so good. Not a murmur,' Kathryn tailed off.

Naila's chuckle at being spoken to had been a reward of sorts, though bitter-sweet. Her mouth became a tiny bow that tied and retied itself at each note. Glenda said, 'That's love-ly. Mm . . . like I said, I've more material for you. Just needs typing in.'

Soon they were cruising towards goodbye. Glenda missed her daughter, missed Kathryn's shiny freckled face that foundation always disappeared off as soon as applied and the energetic gestures that Laurens Harrell must be on receiving end of . . . and then there was an extra piece of cartilage on her left ear. She had been born with it and she, Glenda, was probably the only person on earth who ever noticed now. But Kathryn's loss was safely stowed in a mental file of spoilage, penned in there with the split from Kathryn's father and any thought of his new ménage (containing a recent addition, the little boy he'd always wanted, she supposed). All secure.

The second custard tart seemed to be missing. Glenda wiped her fingers, found Narratives and hit Open.

Unpaid field work: Kathryn's suggestion had been a life-saver though at the time her need hadn't been apparent – until, well, it was absurd. She had never told anyone, not even Marie. Though looking back the danger signals were out. If referred to herself, Glenda would have noted them in the record as slowed reaction times and a tendency to clumsiness and inertia interspersed with manic activity. Post divorce and housemove, work continued in its absorbing, galling way. But in time off she might either emulsion the walls of her bedroom in vibrant pink – or not get up at all. Whole days drained away re-reading from a school career she hadn't particularly enjoyed *Jane Eyre, A Kid for Two Farthings, The Franchise Affair* and *Jamaica Inn*, disparate, mis-ordered, familiar – and weirdly numbing. The only pleasure she seemed capable of was detesting change. A guest house at the end of Rainsdale become a smart little hotel – no, *boutique* hotel – with a mean, lifted face. She avoided it, not the building but the entire road. A stretch of wrought ironwork along her route to the shops was repaired. Missing curlicues, missing for years by the looks of it, had been replaced and rustproofed and Glenda found herself concocting a plan where she bought a single hacksaw blade – it would need to be from one of the superstores in town, not the Windsor Road DIY where she'd already drawn attention for seeking advice on ant killer. The blade part-concealed in her pocket of a full coat, as the evenings closed in she could incise the metal away, a little at a time, work on it between passers-by if she had to. Or go out really late. One night it would snap.

Safer to stop walking the neighbourhood altogether – she put on two dress sizes and was on the way to a third.

Then Kathryn had set her going, a daughter's need managing to eclipse her own.

To re-read her original preface was to blush: *This city*

*makes stories from its subconscious the way uneasy individuals make dreams. They are worked on and get passed around. New ones spring up from a resurrected Cardiff, tales that could not have been told before they gave it an Arts Centre with the poems written on the outside and a football stadium with a Thunderbirds roof. There is one about that roof and a bet and the pair of severed legs that are the result. Teenage boys like to tell it you ...*

All wrong, this sort of approach. She realised now having had it explained: what was required was a certain type of story and its simple reporting. The great Laurens Harrell may be muscling in but, initially, so had she. Kathryn wanted from the researcher only bare data, neither comment nor response and no personalised marginal notes, *thanks Mum.*

'And no names. Just initials for identification of source with sex, age and self-selected racial group.'

But to abstract narrator from narrative seemed perverse. The contributors stayed alive in Glenda's memory long after their stories had been become Word Documents, titled, initialled, turned into attachments and dispatched. Chance meetings could present you with precious nuggets. (The reverse was also true: only recently a local history buff at a school she was visiting had proved a dry hole.) And then there were the circumstances of the telling, what was got from the exchange, how you felt hearing it ... and afterwards, where was the fit? What else in your experience now rubbed up against it and was jostled aside or lost an edge. Glenda found every instinct opposed Kathryn's harsh prescription, each time she brought a fresh specimen home. She wrote two versions now. Always the first was for herself.

## Velma's story

This is my best so far. It's not set in our Brave New Cardiff, so no sliding roof on the sports stadium, no new lagoon made just to be looked at from a thousand balconies. What it has got is an only-in-the-lost-city feel to it. I nabbed it on the sort of warm soggy evening when you could get out there with a net and catch a moth the size of a sparrow. But it would have red eyes on the wings and you'd know it flittered off one of the ships that still tie up here on occasion. An ex-dinner lady told it me, out for a smoke in the bingo interval. Velma said who she was and none of this 'Why d'you want to know?' rubbish. When she saw I'd written VJ on the case label she let out a cackle that could have shattered the community centre windows.

'VJ!' she laughed and elbowed the two on either side of her in the ribs. 'Victory Over Japan! That's what my dad used to call me.' They looked down at their boots, embarrassed the way teenagers are.

I got lucky only because she smoked like me and because a group made up of a grey-haired woman huddled under a canopy with a couple of towering kids, bikers, had to be worth a try. I joined them. I'd had my five for the day. I thought if somebody offers I am going to say yes and take a cigarette but Velma was down to the filter tip in another puff. The others, who she said were her grandson and his girlfriend, didn't smoke. By keeping our backs up against

the pebble dash we could feel the rods of rain just missing
our faces before they hit the gravel. Before long only the
bikers in their leathers would have dry feet. All three of
them would want to be back inside. I explained quick as
I could.

'Bit old for a student, love, aren't you?'

'I'm doing research. Thing is, I'm collecting stories from
all sorts of different people to show what's called common-
ality.'

'Who you callin' common?' Velma demanded.

'No, not at all.'

'I'm jokin', love.'

She understood though. She was the perfect find. Next,
she dismissed the others and off they shuffled back to their
pool table. But I saw them stop in the doorway, just checking, which was nice. I must have passed.


So, Velma's story. It was not long after the Second World
War and Cardiff was yet to become the capital of Wales.
But it was full of human life and industry. The Docks area
was like a funnel with the country's ground-up bones being
poured through it. If it was well past its peak fifty different
nationalities were still rubbing along and getting by. We've
all seen the photographs. 'Gathering the Jewels' they call
it at The Library of Wales. Vacuum-packing the past, my
daughter says. Not much in the way of precious stones in
this Butetown, but most of the kids are clean and fed and
they've got manners fit for the world beyond. But whether
they go or hang on here, the residents <u>don't</u> call it Tiger
Bay.

It's a Sunday. Every religion and none is represented, often in the same household, the same bed. Still, Sunday is special. It means chapel for some, a day of no work for others or just self-medication with drink.

Here is what happened. At around teatime, a boy (he is only five or six) is gone and a wailing woman is walking the length of a Butetown street. The street answers. The little terraces were all standing back then, tight. Better dwellings that had survived were boarding houses so the population is dense and a search party easily mustered. Those who can explain the kafuffle to those without the English or the Welsh to find out for themselves. Every able-bodied man and some women get out there and look for the little lad and keep looking. Darkness threatens. Ahead of many is a fourteen-hour working day. But they carry on, tramping the cobbles, calling out. There are piles of rot to be pried apart and more privy doors to be hammered on. As they go through the woodpiles and derelict warehouses, are the outcomes they're imagining any more innocent than ours would be? Probably not. And always there is the Inner Harbour itself to bother about. It must give a sense and smell of the water that's in wait for any man, woman or especially child.

The little boy is not found. Velma doesn't pretend to be able to name him which is a pity. I like to know. Names can tell you a lot. (I met a little girl called Naila by her Egyptian father and discovered it means 'unbeaten'.) No name though and no mention of the police. Did they seek official help? When I asked the response was just Velma huffing at me. I had said something in bad taste. I hadn't understood.

One man is missing from the search, a widower, a father himself. He would be out with the rest if a brood of his own children weren't keeping him in. Someone ought to let him know. In Velma's telling, 'the woman from the corner' goes to his unlocked door. (Forget all your warm fuzziness here. Locks are expensive and people are poor. They only get broken when drunks come home. Landlords let them stay that way.) So the woman walks straight in and finds him sitting up with an old newspaper in a foreign language someone has given him. He's big and bulky as his own shadow from the lamp. It takes a while but at last he understands. And an expression crosses his face that the woman says she will never forget. She follows him up the stairs without invitation.

There is a back room and a pair of bedsteads. Children are fast asleep in each, heads top and bottom. Under the blankets their little feet can be made out, plaited together like the tails of tinned fish. Girls in one, boys in the other. But there's something about the left-hand bed, something not right. This picture must have bided its time in the father's brain and now makes a wrinkle on his forehead. There's a lack of symmetry about the arrangement. On the pillow there's an extra mop of hair.

Just like in all the best stories we come to the Three Questions.

'Did the child not mind being fed with the others?'

Of course not. Food was a pretty welcome event in any child's day.

'And did the child not object at being bathed along with the rest of the boys in water already used for the girls?'

Oh, yes. They all did, every time the bath came out. The boys never got used to it. They never liked it any better than first time it was done to them.

'But surely he made a fuss at being put to bed in a strange room in a strange house?'

All children fretted at bedtime, didn't they? The little cuckoo no more and no less than most.

I don't think I will ever get a better one than this. It says the past isn't another country. Then, as now, a child was a piece of currency that could fall into good hands or bad. But nothing could take the worth out of it. Velma's story dips into our worst nightmares and comes out with a ladle of Golden Syrup. What surprises me is how much I want it to be true.

The pair of legs that fall onto the Stadium's touchline when the roof opens? A man who fixed my car told it me again last week and it's still just a locker-room joke. But the child, fast asleep in the crowded bed, I want him to be real. I want him to have survived and be somewhere in the city to this day. He'd be an old man, a grandfather himself maybe, walking the barrage and looking across to a Butetown he can barely recognise. Everywhere big hotels have sprung up and the apartments with their glass doors might as well contain Martians for all he knows. On the new lagoon there are boats out there worth more than his house – even if he owns one. I like to think it's a wonderful day. The sun will be dazzling off the copper cowl of the Millennium building that's shaped like a hill. And I'd <u>love</u> him to be saying to whoever he's with, 'When I was a kid I lived round here.'

❧

She has fallen asleep in the chair she realises. One second Glenda can feel the tip of her finger as it describes the fold of extra cartilage in Baby Kathryn's left ear, the next she is saying into her phone, 'Yes! Hello?' Her cheek feels sore from being peeled off her arm.

'Hiya,' Marie Raglan says. 'Sorry it's late.' She gives a soft laugh. A noise in the background tells Glenda she isn't alone. When there is no response, she adds, 'you all right then, love?'

'Yes-s. Fine. Thanks. Well, you know . . . it was about Ashley Foulkes.' Marie groans from across the Bay. Soon she will be gone to join a new Substance Abuse Intervention Team and for the first time Glenda senses her friend's disengagement. They will see each other rarely with fewer cases to bind their interest. Marie has a man in her life, too, by the sound of it, a man who is close and restless. Some small object makes a soft landing next to the phone. 'OK – yes, her again. But I was at Ashley's – got in, as well! – this afternoon and . . . it's nothing I can pin down. It's there though. Talk to me for a minute, will you? Can I tell you?' And before Marie decides she says, 'I just don't want it to end bad.'

# SETTLED AT CIVEEN

What else could she do?

She said it out loud to Marc as she caught him in the kitchen, the glasses rattling on the tray, the popped beer bottles stuck on three fingers of his spare hand.

'Nothing,' he said. The back and forth of a dozen conversations next door made it unnecessary for the lowering of their voices. 'You don't have to do anything. It's going fine.'

'More food, do you think? I could get out those pattie-things. I could start them heating up before I go round with the –'

'If you like. If you want to.' He stared vaguely around the huge cupboarded room. Lines of bottles and bowls covered every horizontal surface. In the deep butler's sink, where ice cubes were forgotten and dissolving into a reservoir of water, his eyes seemed to find focus on a single, savoury biscuit. It rotated slowly in the icy eddies. 'But to be honest, there's enough food out there to break the Famine.'

'Are you mad? Don't say that! For God's sake don't let anyone hear you saying that.'

He laughed, a real laugh that gave a glimpse of black

nostril hair and strong level teeth. His Adam's apple bobbed. Marc Farina was a big man and tended to use his body to communicate his mood. Now the tray's compliment of filled glasses jostled each other, the reds overflowing – and her husband's long, tanned face flushed ruby from cheekbone to shadowed jaw. 'Calm down.' A deep voice, a voice that was calming in itself but most hearers would be more intrigued by the accent: impossible to place. 'Tristan Da Cunha,' Sam had heard him say once – in London, not long after they first met – and he had been believed. He gestured now with his head. 'Come on and meet this potter who's married to Bill. Orla, her name is. I've just told her you're a painter. Come on. I've just told her you and Sam'll get on like a house on fire –'

'Don't put it like that,' she begged but she followed him out.

'Out' was to a wide galleried hall whose period could be judged by the weight and diameter of the timbers and a lack of right angles – but the wood gleamed because newly oiled and the plaster was repaired and freshly painted. It contained only a pair of Danish teak tables against opposing walls, three very jazzy modern canvases in acrylic – and around three-dozen guests. These ranged in age from twenty to sixtyish, were male and female in couples mainly and with some grown-up children. An hour into the entertainment, they were heated – if anything, overheated – settled in, drinking wine or beer and eating a score of different titbits off antique meat plates that passed beneath their fingers, as regular as tube trains. Aside from the host and hostess, the part-time girl from Anderson's was helping out with feeding and watering. *She*, Martine, knew everyone present, which was more than Sam did – and Sam couldn't help but feel it was Martine and Marc (even the names were euphonious) that were responsible for the total lack of awkwardness, the early slide into button-loosening ease that a long-established group can achieve in even unfamiliar territory.

Above the scent of food and drink and old-fashioned soaps and a variety of perfumes, including her own, Sam, could detect another characteristic odour being emitted by some of the assembled. It was tea towel, the essence of clothes laundered and then *nearly* dried several times over before finally succumbing to the drying process. Clean-damp, to her mind, instantly distinguishable from the dirty-damp of a dishcloth, say, and it rose now on the warmth of scrubbed bodies. They were in the largest space the house had to offer. It was a fitting one for this celebratory party, thrown as thanks for all involved in the restoration of the eighteenth century building – in particular the hall. Once several rooms, now it was a fine, lofty expanse occupying the entire central cottage in the row. Over two hundred flags of reclaimed limestone (each carefully chosen for the richness of its patina and then polished by special gadget come up from Cork) kept at bay the late November chill with a warmth generated beneath. But the new oak staircase glowed of itself. Snaking down from the darkness, first it bisected the gathering and then, with a graceful and feminine turn that replicated the exposed chimney arch, lined up with a widened front door. John Hayes, the joiner, stood proprietarily at its newel post;

his wife stood beside him and beside her their son (also a John). The younger man was astonishingly beautiful with sculptured full lips and pierced brows, Sam had already noticed. Needing not a second for conscious thought, she veered away from this little group-within-a-group.

John Hayes could only be mortified at what had been added, just this week, to his flight of seventeen wide blond treads.

'Orla Bowsie, my wife Sam.'

She found herself shaking hands with a wiry redhead considerably older than herself, whose thin wrist barely retained a pair of jade bracelets. There was once a pretty girl and a pretty woman, Sam suspected, and her eyes were still a striking feature, luminous and very blue. But odd, deep crevices now marred the face. As well as the expected crows' feet and frown lines, two deep verticals lay beneath the cheek bones and two more horizontals bridged the neat nose – as though she were in the habit of doing something unpredictable with her expression. Mrs Bowsie . . . the potter . . . yes, the alibi of creativity was being brought in to cover shiny black trousers, still creased from the hanger across the knees, and a polychrome blouse many sizes too big. Her hennaed hair was shorter than Marc's, her mottled neck had lost its battle with wind and sun.

'Orla! You're Bill's wife? He's made a wonderful use of the space, don't you think so?' Sam could register her own, over-bright tone but too late, much too late, for modulation. 'So clever.' (Bill Bowsie from nearby Castleisland had drawn up the plans for what was known locally as the *boarding out*, adding an extra storey into the roof of Civeen

Farm.) 'This *was* the middle cottage you know. Well – it's
obvious I suppose. The other cottage has the sitting room
with my mother's bedroom over it and . . . that left us the
barn. A lovely, *huge* kitchen – you must go and have a look,
please just walk around. A garden room and Marc's study
beyond that . . . then there's our bedroom up above, bathrooms and a studio for me. We love it. Please tell him how
much we love it, won't you? Where is he by the way, oh
that's him with – over there –'

Orla Bowsie's smile owned up to a missing tooth
beyond the canine. She sipped her Pinot Noir. Whatever
was responsible for those lines it was nothing simple as
smiling. She was totally composed – enough to leave a long
pause before saying, 'So you're an artist?'

'A graphic designer by training. But you see, we've travelled a lot since we were married. London – America, twice.
Now here. I do some freelancing . . . the acrylics are a new
thing.'

Orla Bowsie happened to be facing one of Sam's painting, a riot of rose madder and viridian and puce, it was
called *Valentia*. It was scrutinised, title, signature, everything, close-to . . . from a step back. 'Oh, you're an Orphist,
Sam, born out of your time. Yes? Now I have at home a
Sonia Delaunay plate – a porcelain plate in the original
box. You'd like it.' The name meant something to Sam but
not a something that was usable. When she said she was
sure she would, Orla pressed on with 'So your man Grayson
Perry, now . . . what's that about?'

'Yes! *I know*' had to do. Sam fled to where Marc's broad
back offered a reference point. As the merits of nearby

towns were being gone through by the cluster around him, the familiar muscle-mounds beneath the green cloth of his shirt rose and fell at each arm movement. She had a strong impulse to press her cheek into that landscape and close her eyes against a pressure that seemed to be forcing them forward in her skull. 'No! We'll go into Castleisland for day to day stuff,' Marc was saying. 'During most of the week we're in Dublin anyway, but for choice it's Killarney with me. What a place, Killarney! I can't get enough of it. You can buy anything you want, get a decent meal – and you can swim it all off again in the lake!' He struck his own midriff as an illustration: no tremors beneath the impact on the green shirt. Though he was over fifty and the head greying, at his throat the visible tufts were black and the neck muscles firm.

'And have you, Marc? Have you swum in it?' Bill Bowsie asked.

'Yes! In the Lower Lake, I have.'

A loud and sincere cheer went up and Bill Bowsie play-punched Marc's upper arm. During the restoration he'd called Marc *Mr Farina*. Now he play-punched his former client's bicep and shouted, 'He's after swimming in the lake!'

What filled the lake was running purposefully down three uncurtained hall windows. It was properly dark and nasty-looking out there and yet the guests' solid-seeming reflections confounded the visual sense; they stood out in it, unconcerned and dry, throwing back heads exposed to the elements as they threw nuts into their mouths or drink. What a pity she'd forgotten to switch on the wall lamps along the gallery before anyone arrived: they would have shone against the raw umber as welcome. To do it now would draw attention to . . . something – to the passage of time, perhaps. It might be taken as a hint to leave even though coats were hung in a small room beside the kitchen door . . . the aspiration to *swank*, that must be avoided. But of course she hadn't forgotten the lamps, the ever-corrective, supervisory section of herself pointed out. A light up there might be disturbing – to someone.

The stiff northerly that had made just unloading the car an ordeal in the afternoon now became a ballista to pelt the face of Civeen. Although several of the guests had walked up from the village beneath umbrellas of varying degrees of tattiness, only Sam gave the outside more than a glance. The modest plus points of Killarney, Tralee and other Kerry towns were still being knocked back and to. All were for Killarney. Very stylish, very *sophisticated* it was suggested (although nobody used the word). Hanging on there to New Ireland. And it was. Silently Sam found herself in agreement whilst at the same instant came the vivid recollection of her last outing.

. . . Never a confident driver, the manoeuvre of getting off St Margaret's and onto Rock Road had just been completed and her beautiful new bag (an early present from Marc) lay on the car seat beside her, the list of items unobtainable locally tucked into it. She had glanced down at the prize once, twice, gloatingly – looked up and there the mid-morning traffic was hiccupping to a halt. A wave of judders and red tail lights swept backwards. She had to stand almost on the brake feeling the seatbelt's grip and a comb tumbled into her lap that should have held newly-washed hair. Through the pale curtain of it, she saw them: a pack of loose dogs. A dozen strong, they cavorted through the vehicles, a huge shaggy monster in the lead, animals of every size and conformation in pursuit. On they came, jostling, shoulder-charging their neighbours, parting around a motorcyclist, brushing against his booted foot planted on the tarmac, reforming as they swept past. As if by group consent they made for the narrow canyon between her own and the car ahead and were funnelled through it, one pie-bald collie flinging itself into the air above a slower leader, the light body of the Fiat registering the soft surge of their passage. Hardly had the collie made landfall than it mounted a thin brown lurcher, come slinking along beside. The writhing rejection scattered the pack members and their snarls erupted and spread into primate-like yelling. Terrible injuries . . . the ripping of pelts was threatened and the exposing of flesh – when suddenly they were gone. She found she could exhale. Having negotiated and contributed to the chaos of the High Street-St Anne's Road junction (without losses), they disappeared into a side turning. The last glimpse she had of the pack it was elongated with desperate intent, back on the bitch's trail. And from amongst the stationary vehicles, still not a horn had been blown, not a window been wound down, not voice raised.

'And how's your mother liking it with us?' Angie Moore was asking her from very close to. Sam saw the untasted wine in her own glass flinch although Angie's face was all smoothed out with kindliness.

'Oh – yes. She does. Thank you.'

'A great thing, having her with you – and now you'll be all three together in time for Christmas. I must have a word with her before I go.'

'Well –'

'You've no other family, you said?'

'No. I mean, step-sons. Marc has two sons. From his first marriage.'

'Oh yes.'

'She died.'

'So she did.'

Angie seemed relatively satisfied but the woman with her – a small tubby unknown woman with a hand clutching a shoulder bag – maintained an eager stare.

'She was killed in a car crash. In Buenos Aires.'

'Oh, God love her!' the stranger whispered.

'They have very dangerous roads – in Buenos Aires. In Argentina, in fact,' Sam said. It was what had been said to her by Marc when the news of Pilar's death had arrived. 'The most dangerous roads in South America,' she added for good measure. It could be true.

'Now isn't that terrible?'

'Yes. It is.'

'And those poor boys –'

'They live with their grandparents. They're at school. Marc thinks – well, there's the Technological University . . . of Argentina. Marc thinks in a couple of years –'

'Ah, the poor little souls.'

But Angie came to the rescue. 'Sam, was it you that'll be thirty-eight next birthday or was that Martine's sister? *Yes*

*I'm watching you Martine – stop giving my husband that Black Bush.* It was never you was going to be forty, was it? I've been through that one. Don't let it get you down. (No, that *was* Martine's sister.) I'd say you were just like me when you were a little girl. Never imagined being thirty never mind forty, did you? Or if you did, did you ever think –'

It was as though curiosity was added to the Kerry mains: even Dublin ran with a more decent interest quotient than here, out west. Angie Moore was a music teacher, someone Sam had had down as a possible friend – this despite Angie's huge following of children. That had been over a year ago, when Marc first bought the house and surrounding land. Angie was married to Dev, the stonemason, but a professional man through and through, a man with a poetic take on artisanship. Dev the Obscure, she and Marc had christened him between themselves. His long-delayed response to any enquiry often included an idiosyncratic usage or a learned reference at odds with the hoary denims and the knuckles high with scar tissue. But now Angie was pregnant again with twins – joyfully pregnant – with a couple more babies to add to her four. *Horrible*, at her age. To have *one* child so late in life was wickedly self-indulgent. Sam could barely bring herself to look at Angie, lowering her body carefully onto the next to bottom step, the drink slopping, nevertheless, over the half-barrel of flowered smock.

'I'll bet she's for enjoying herself, your Ma! Did she not tell you I met her in Anderson's the week after she came over the water?' Orla Bowsie had approached under cover of Angie's mass and now joined them. 'Are you doing OK there, Angie?'

*Met her in Anderson's.*

'Shouldn't I go and get you a fruit juice? Fizzy water?' Sam tried.

'*No*. I'm into the last trimester. It never did the others any harm. I've told the midwife, forget the epidural. Purce Rennie's out on the golf course when you need him anyway. I'm having these two under Beaujolais and Beethoven. I've got my iPod packed. 'The Moonlight' for the run-up, 'The Violin Concerto' for the last act. Bom-*bum*. Bom bar-bum, bom-*bum* bom bar-bum!' She mimed a wide-legged push to time. 'I'll have to rely on Dev for the bottle, he's to smuggle it in. You were saying about your mother –'

'Irene,' Orla Bowsie added helpfully. 'We had a good old talk.'

'She's – she's not very well, you know?' In SW6 this would have been more than sufficient. But all three women remained fixed on her, alert, receptive. She tried a gesture somewhere beyond Angie's bulk. They waited. 'Will you just excuse me a moment? I think I left the oven on high . . .' But there was an involuntary glance up into the darkness, a poor bluffer's tell. She wove through her guests.

*Now come on now Marc, you've lived in New York, you're an educated man – is it not the case that hundreds of years ago where Ground Zero is now, there was this terrible massacre of the Indians by the colonists? And – no it's true, the fellow writing the piece had been looking into this sort of thing –*

*Of course Purce is coming! Three weeks, we reckon. And we'll be playing a round at each one, grading everything as we go – the course, club house facilities . . . bar!*

*And here's a thing – Baron Von Munchausen, the Baron Von Munchhausen, yes? The fellow wrote the books . . . and they made the film? He actually died in Killarney. Well just outside Killarney, in Muckross. He did! And he was still at it, he was still telling tales. He pretended he was one of those mining engineers and he's getting a nice little retainer off some local landowner to look for gold. Yes, exactly. He did! But if you're not finding anything, then you might just as well be not finding gold as not finding lead!*

*Lovely dog, too! Pax, we've called him. John didn't want to take him in but I said it's bad luck to turn away anything, man or animal, that comes to your door. I'll be bringing him to the Puck Fair.*

*Oh the fair! But I've always thought it was very hard on the goat.*

*Farina, now, that's a lovely name –* it was her own name but Sam kept moving – *I was just saying Mrs Farina, oh she's not heard me – I was just saying – oh, Angie, have you named these next two yet, because I was just saying to – I was just saying Farina, now, that's nice enough for a first name – for a girl.*

She had remembered, of course, to turn down the oven: barely warm to the touch, its contents – but always better than burnt. What looked like miniature dumplings but exuding a sharp, undumpling scent were tipped out anyway onto *The Upland Cottage,* the rest onto *Noon at Blackwater Bridge.* But when they were arranged and the golden crumbs swept from the plates' edges, her attention was dragged away by the outside howling. A mixed weight of air and water was barging towards them from the direction of Shannon. *Had closed the airport at Shannon,* she'd heard someone say. It had been the last thing said as she made her escape, *So our Christy is coming though, well they'll be getting diverted to Dublin – though we can only hope it's to be Cork – oh Joseph, he's five now, a fine fella –*

Something solid, twig or rubbish, lashed itself against the back door, rattling the handle. A moment and Marc joined her. Rigid, turned from him and not turning around, she could always be seeming to check her reflection in the microwave's glass.

'Don't bother. You look fine.'

'You're getting an Irish accent now. It's less than two years!'

This he took as a challenge. 'Well you didn't like Poughkeepsie. That's good isn't it?' His nature was protean as his history, Italian/Welsh with a dash of the Argentine as he always introduced himself. More than a dash she would never say, that leaves behind a wife who goes and dies and two teenage sons.

She teased her arranged-tousle of hair. 'I've forgotten to put out olives.' Mistiming it, her rings clanked against the jar she took down.

'What's wrong?'

'I don't know.' It wasn't a lie. Possibilities suggested themselves but she didn't *know*. The finishing of the house, was it, and the ending of a project? The realisation that this was it. After all the flitting back and forth across the Atlantic, this was to be their stopping place. Ireland. When they'd married he'd said *There's a place in Kerry that suits me – would suit us. I'll show it you. You can fish and sail and walk the Reeks*... Now there was a white Dublin apartment and Civeen. And these people, their families. All of them – and: 'They keep asking about Pilar – oh and Mother.'

'They're interested, that's all. Family's a big thing here. That's how they are.'

'Oh, they've taken to my mother. Even though she's English.'

*'For God's sake Sam!'*

'No, no . . .' she understood completely his exasperation, shared it. 'They'll be wondering why she's not down.'

'Rubbish. Getting on for eighty? And you've only to look at her to see how frail she is. Too much, all this.'

But who had this alibi just been used on – before herself?

Some actual uproar was reaching its climax in the hall. A man's voice cried, 'Whoa there! I told you so, Bill!' and a woman's high rejoinder was so shrill, so near a scream, as to be without words, though everybody was laughing, calling out 'There you go!' and 'Right, right!'

Sam shrugged. 'I just couldn't stand it. You know how she'd be. That Orla-woman had come across her in Anderson's Bar. She just smirked when she said it – so I'd know. She'll have seen her all made-up, the wig, the heels, the complete thing – and absolutely wrecked. I bet it was the night Purce Rennie *just happened* to drop in and brought her back with him, because they all talk, don't they?'

He took her in his arms and pulled her close, the jar of olives painful and cold between them. 'They don't think that much of it here. John Hayes brought an old uncle to the Ring of Kerry dinner. He told the bluest jokes I've ever heard in my life. Very *gauchesco*.' She wouldn't do it. Wouldn't pick up his smile, his mood and try running with it. 'Anyway she's asleep –'

'I put a pill – no, actually, I put two pills in her brandy. After she ate. You said we didn't have time for coffee with them coming for nine, so I gave her the brandy . . . and just the two diazepam.'

He blinked – just two blinks – but she could see close, reasoning thought and a careful picking out of words from those in his head. 'It was a big brandy. I saw it. Is that safe?'

'She been on the pills for years. I've watched her wash a lot stronger stuff down with whatever's going. I'm amazed anything works. You don't know her, Marc. You don't really know her, not the way I do. And I'm sorry but I don't care about somebody's old uncle. It's *worse* in a woman. When I was growing up –'

'Bit of a nightmare, uh-huh.'

'And having her with us – here. In this house. Twenty years – but nothing's changed because people don't change, do they? You just get more of what they always were coming out. So – she's more like Irene than Irene used to be. What did I expect?'

'It was only September. That's no time at all. We knew –

we talked about it. But there wasn't anywhere else. It was the right thing to do.'

She could almost think this was an appeal. He was a big, capable, managing type of man who went from country to country putting things right, combating chaos. It was easy to envisage the monster chaos flying from Marc: Civeen had been an aftermath of a building, its walls sprouting, its roof plastic and tin sheet. *Too far gone*, she had said when he brought her over to see it, first – but he had had it put right. Now the night could rage beyond the double glazing: on the windowsill the pot of basil failed to stir.

'Let's see how we fare before we-'

'We make any decisions, yes,' she echoed and embellished, letting her head sink. Maybe his continued hold wasn't all for her. Pilar had been raised from the dead by a stranger's question. But for Marc she was probably always lurking, waiting in ambush. When he was distracted or thwarted or just jet-lagged, out she came. And Pilar's children. A pair of young men, soon. Their reach would lengthen, now she and Marc had this home to offer. Now they were *settled*. Handsome, dark young men who were only images as yet would walk up Dev Moore's stone steps with accusing eyes and have to be let in. A disreputable Mother was nothing measured against two abandoned boys. 'You're good,' she whispered. 'You're better than me with her. Not that you'll ever get a word of thanks. You just manage it – somehow . . . you're good.'

'Mr Perfect, I think you mean. Anyway, easier for me. I didn't have to weather growing up with Irene. Come on –'

He rubbed big flattened palms up and down her sleeves' silk as though chafing away the cold. 'Don't miss the party.'

'What if I can't bear it? Her being here.'

'Then we'll think of something else. Let it happen first.'

'I could put another box of these things in –'

'Or not.'

Angie Moore was still holding court to a semi-circle of wives. Sam skirted them, squared her shoulders and made for where John Hayes stood talking to his son and another small but tough-looking man. This man's wide pink face jerked up and down much oftener than was needed to signal agreement with the speaker . . . she had an unclear memory of the face. It had appeared at the beginning of the work with a machine to – to dig out drains. All three were drinking Murphy's from straight glasses which she managed to top up from the single bottle she had brought. In her other hand were the tepid falafels. 'Have you had something to eat? Has Martine been looking after you?'

'Yes, yes,' said John Junior, that generous mouth mobile . . . correctness . . . smirk.

'I have,' said his father, 'but Terry here, he can't get enough of those things you're holding, Mrs Farina.'

Terry was caught mid-nod. He looked at the Hayeses, looked at Sam, took a falafel and placed it in his mouth.

'Glad you like them. Terry.'

The noise was airport-terminal level and the gale and external drama was near drowned-out by competing voices, goading each other to up the volume, up the pitch or be lost. Somewhere behind her there was a snatch of duet: *When Michaelmas comes round again/ oh then I shall have money!* Followed by *Yes!* and *No! No!* and when the lights flickered as cables strung along the lane clashed, no one paused in speech, laughter or their rendition of *I'll put it in a yew tree box and give it to my honey!*

Glad you like them. She was glad, *really* glad, the Hayes father and son had drifted to this far corner, away from the staircase and its customising. The centre of the hall was completely occupied by women, she saw now, while the males formed a grey and brown fringe around them. Terry proved the exception in his red shirt and unusual tie . . . A very unusual tie of painted silk, when Sam looked closely. It sported a *naked* Madonna. Marc had vanished though she heard his deep confident laugh from a distance and suspected he was showing off the toys decking out his study to Bill Bowsie and some of the others. 'Another of these?' she demanded of the masticating Terry. He shook his head – no! – and John Junior snorted. Unnerved she wished Marc *could just stay in the room, he's the host isn't he, all these people here, hardly knowing some of them from Adam because he was the one kept coming over when it was all going on, no point in driving for hours and having some geriatric bricklayer explaining that was fine just fine but he'd rather wait for Mr Farina, have a word at the weekend so they could be making a decision . . .*

Perhaps it was the absence of Marc that stilled the conversation. The big man, an extrovert with one foot always on the podium, was always leaving a gathering quietened and lessened by his departure. Silence, in the room, just for an instant: and the wind had dropped, unless –

In the lull you could hear the motor come to life up

on the unlighted gallery. Most of those assembled below heard it and glanced toward the sound.

Irene always did enjoy making an entrance. She glided down into view, not so much sitting on the stair lift as hunched. Her mottled knees were beneath her chin, her bare fleshless legs wrapped in strap arms, with the points of each elbow lost in the padding of the chair to afford some stability. Between a pair of curled, bird's feet the sparse white frizz of her pubis was visible – as though she had sat down absent-mindedly on a small albino pet.

'Oh, good Lord!' This from Orla Bowsie. Quick-wittedly she hauled Angie Moore upright (no easy task but deftly accomplished) and so out of Irene's path.

'*Samantha!*' Irene called as soon as she could focus on her daughter's face amongst the many faces tipped toward her. 'I'm having the oddest dream. I keep hearing people singing. Is there a party?' She took in the rosy illumination from shaded sconces, the evergreens and bronze chrysan-themums in vases on each of the windowledges and tables, the guests, the crystal glasses in the grasp of the guests, the food half-raised to the open mouths of the guests – and smiled. When both hands fluttered up to her hair (a gesture identical to that performed by Sam in the kitchen a quarter hour earlier) the silk chemise, her only garment, rode up also to the region of her waist.

Every male eye in the room was turned on his drink.

Orla had the Pashmina off Angie and around Irene before Sam moved. 'I suppose this thing goes in reverse, does it Sam?' she demanded.

'What? *Yes*, I'll do it. It's this . . . I think.' The mechanism was new, the controls unfamiliar. Her fingers felt like someone else's. 'There.'

The three ascended in unison, Orla's arm around Irene's shoulders, step by slow step, Sam at her heels.

Into the darkness.

Irene, bemused and yawning, consented to have the nightdress pulled back over her head.

'She says she can't get out of this on her own – usually. Oh, Mother!'

Over Orla's bent back, Sam examined Irene – for something, anything, to respond to in her mother's face. Since lacking the frame of the platinum wig that was shining out cruelly on its stand, all she could observe was how far that face had seeped backwards over the years. Once so vivid, so definite, so hard, now Irene's hairline was scarcely marked out by the first few grey tufts. It was wandering in the direction of her high crown. Little lemon ears had been left stranded in patches of smooth skin as additional facial features.

Orla tutted. 'Don't you worry about it.' Expertly she flipped Irene's pillow, smoothed it and stroked the older woman's temples as she lay back. 'There you go now, Irene.' Sam watched in amazement at her mother's lop-sided but genuine smile . . . her drowsy nod of the head. 'You get a good night's sleep. That'll see you right. Now how would it be if I came round in the morning? Shall I do that, shall I? We'll have a bit of a party ourselves, me and you. I'll bring us a cake.'

Sam saw there was the option of a shared glance, a laugh that could erupt from either and bring a cosy emotional up-welling to enfold the standing pair. Almost Orla's fingers touched hers as the folds in the quilt were undone, the creases pushed to the corners and extinction. But Sam kept her chin tightly in and was the first to step away from the bedside. 'Thank you. Well – thanks.' On the landing she paused for the reassuring snap of her mother's door catch.

Half-way down and the room raised its head to them. Sam tried to focus on a painting of Rough Point with its egg-yolk sky and orange sea. A scorching afternoon, they had had, Marc striding along the headland, the ocean itself calm, the surfers driven off the water by the flat of it. All before Civeen was half complete. Before Irene. Orla said, 'I was just telling Sam here about *our* house-warming Bill.'

Bill Bowsie, with Marc, was returned and among the happy few who'd missed the show. 'I was saying, d'you remember I sat down on Ryan Quigley's knee? He said he could guess my weight but my waters broke and I damn near drowned your man.' Orla, through high animation, came out suddenly in all her truly magnetic charm. The exposed vacancy in the upper jaw, the bunches of garish cotton across the flat chest, the nipples managing to push up through the cotton now, hard as those olives still in their jar, none of it mattered. And the eccentric lines . . . the lines were revealed as conduits of Orla's signature affection: carnival.

Everybody roared. Most tried to catch Bill Bowsie's eye, leering and shaking their heads before turning away. And there was Martine back as soon as she wasn't needed, joining in as though she were a guest, her lipstick smeared, her hand on Purce Rennie's forearm. Why was Purce Rennie here anyway?

'Don't you get me going, Orla,' shouted Angie Moore across them all. 'It could happen again. Are you with me Purce? I might christen your house for you, Sam. *Sam!* I might christen your house for you – and then where would you be?'

# ROOF

It has to be perfect.

The construction needs to be practical and its meaning open, readable by anyone who uses it. Material is crucial. Not just the stuff itself – consider its provenance, the connections. With each element immaculate, the whole can be transformed, cut free from the act of making.

He's reading from a very old report, recently obtained, on his chosen quarry: *Welsh slate, for hardness, is unsurpassed . . . The Ancients sometimes roofed with Marble . . . the expense of the material, cost of labour being of no account. The use of Tiles for Roofing purposes may be based upon the fact that they are more artistic than Slates, but those who have built with Tiles, in search of the Artistic, have often found that they have grasped at the shadow and lost the substance.* Extraordinary. An auditor's report that included this sort of language. He angles his stylus for annotation. *Slate can appear,* he adds, *almost* he crosses out almost, *funereal when damp. It is a magical stone nonetheless . . .* nonetheless?

But the stylus drops from his fingers and the NoteBook slides to the carpet.

*We are creatures of stone.*

The idea came to him, strange and complete, just on the point of wakefulness. It came from somewhere – a cold somewhere, by the feel of it. Probably the after effects of a drenching he'd got as he cycled from the station, very late. Later than promised, for sure and not that long before going to sleep. So it was a message to himself, from himself. *Are you hearing me? I'm not satisfied . . . I'm down-right unhappy. Yes, actually, now you mention it, I would like to say something else. No, not a message. I'd like to make a complaint.*

Easily answered, though. That drenching was hours ago. Pull the exposed portions of the self – feet, calves, one cheek of arse and the right arm – under the blanket. Return them to the host. Chafe briskly to welcome home. And again. Now flip over to face the smouldering logs in the grate. Even through closed lids their glow pierces the dark.

*Better?*

*Warmer . . . and, yes, much better, now.*

*Relaxing?*

*Mmm . . . . Actually, no complaints.*

The well-worn chair is surprisingly comfortable, the dawn on the other side of the curtains only tentative. His skin's numbness peels away easily with kneading, gives ground to languor, to heaviness . . . and sleep. Sleep was still there, was in touching distance when: *Before iron, prob-ably before antler and tusk, by the virtues of stone animals were killed and butchered, bellies filled. Flint, shale, slate all had their uses. They named an age.*

He sat up in disgust. Opened his eyes. *Butchered?* How

had that got in there? *The virtues of stone* – well OK, but *butchery?*

'Yori!' It was *her* voice. 'Are you up? I'm coming in.'

'What?' The tartan rug, accommodating only a moment ago, turned traitor. Having covered his entire body it became inadequate to pull around his waist. A fringe caught in the chair's handle became a hitch and the reclining mechanism reversed, shot him upright. On his feet now, with the rug sarong-like, the garment undid its own knot in an instant. His mother entered the room and was treated to the globes of bare buttocks as he groped around his own ankles. 'Hang on. I'm –'

'Don't worry,' she said. On her way through to the kitchen, which had no door but a door-shaped hole that had been plastered around – a poor job, he'd noticed last night – she flicked on the harsh overhead bulb. 'You fell asleep with the light on. I had to come and do it . . . and that's nothing I haven't seen before.'

He heard water running, the kettle being filled. Speculated about whether he could get into his stiff-looking jeans before her return. Just made it.

'So,' she said as they sat with a pine table between them, the tea pot between them, their five-year separation between them, 'you were going to tell me what you've been up to.'

'Busy.'

'Good.'

'Building things.'

'Such as?'

'Well –' *ah, the bird-brightness of those eyes.* '– before I

came away, I started a new project. Just got the go-ahead
– the finance, you know? It's for a path.'

Her mouth – it was still a shapely mouth, a perfect design
for a mouth, still a girl's mouth though she was approaching fifty – lifted at each corner. 'Oh, a *path*.' He was glad to
see that mouth disappear behind her mug.

'Not just a path. Obviously. As I said, it's all part of the
regeneration scheme. Long overdue, huh?' *Come on! You
could manage a nod. It was your town once.* 'This – the one
I'm making, it connects two other . . . key elements. They're
both on the Promenade. It's where most of the funding is
for, obviously, the priority areas. From the bridge, up West
Parade, East Parade and nearly as far as Marine Drive,' he
prompted as though she may have forgotten. *You walked me
along there hundreds of times. To the beach, the shops – later
on, to school.* 'The path's important.' *That's why it's important.* 'Because of the structures it links – and also because
of what it is in itself.'

She was considering. For one heady moment he thought
she was going to express actual interest, *These elements,
say, are they things you've had a hand in?* His pulse accelerated. He framed his reply. But beyond the kitchen window,
where it was getting naturally light, a dog began to bark. It
was joined by another and then another in a rousing dogs'
chorus. His mother pushed back her stool almost upending
his half-full cup. 'Their breakfast's imminent.'

'I'm thinking of slate for it,' he said hurriedly. 'For
various reasons. It cleaves beautifully, wafer thin if you
need. But'll stand immense pressure. It's *formed* under
pressure, so . . . and it's local. Six good quarries in North

Wales, still. I've found a really special one over in Pant-dreiniog.' She had her boots on now, was looking around for something to pull over her black T and leggings. The thick waves of hair, glinting red and silver, were pushed back in impatience as she searched. Her face turned from him, she could've passed for sixteen. 'There are two seams of it, one purple and one blue. I like that, two shades from the same quarry. I thought mix them, you can get the feel of their layers, their nature, from something like that. Mix them, cut them absolutely exactly, of course, then –' he saw her pounce on some fallen object behind the industrial-size waste bin. '– there's the other aspect of it, the one where you're thinking slate, yes, protective,' his gesture was a steeple, up in the air, 'but *whoa!*' Now a halt signal. 'Look. It's being used for something under your feet, for a foundation.'

A black sweater was what she straightened up with. 'Sounds good. Are you coming to give me a hand?'

'Of course. I'll get something else on.'

She was collecting brightly coloured plastic bowls from their overnight soak in the steel sink. They prompted, 'There'll be something in the cupboard behind you – if you want it.'

'Yes. Thanks.'

He found her when she was almost finished. As she gathered up the empties from off the concrete yard, dogs of every size and variety milled around her – but nothing pale and nothing long-coated. He drew attention to the fact and was told these sleeker, darker ones were the hardest to rehome. Light and fluffy, they were what was prized. One tragic-eyed monster stood as high as her hip bones, another smaller thing skittered around on two front legs and a single hind, like a trick it kept on performing and you kept on expecting to miscarry. It shrank from his touch. 'How many are there?'

'Nine at the moment. Bilbo here – that's the lab cross – he's off down the road on Monday. I've found him a place. Going to live in *Henley on Thames*. Going up in the world.'

'Uh-huh.' The smell of the dogs strengthened in their excitement and rose up, a corn chip and motel bed combination with a hint of nettles. They wove around, behind his back which he hated, hitting him, circling and jostling for his mother's attention, nosing her hands. Three-legs showed its teeth. The monster whimpered. Otherwise the canine tension became sub vocal – worse than their racket. 'And now – what next?'

She smiled properly, fully, this time. 'I don't know. Whatever you'd like. I do the chickens, usually.'

Out here in the kind, dull morning her face was a pallid oval, hovering above her black collar, aged, certainly, but still with every ingredient – brows, jawline, angle of nostrils, freckling across the nose, that small mole – shockingly familiar. They were the best known features in the world, his own included. Together they walked from the modern timber kennels and wired dogs runs, to a further brick outhouse: nineteen thirties, probably, which was the bungalow's age. No other structures showed above the thick hedge that together with the buildings hemmed them about. Just a clearing sky and in the distance, trees. 'Do you like it, living here?'

'Oh, yes.'

What did he expect to get back – *no*? In fact, what did he want? Never mind all that about passing for sixteen, she'd had him at sixteen, had toughened to the task of a child – of him – at sixteen. Half his own age now . . . While she fiddled with the rusted finger-latch he took a proper survey of where he'd come to after dark and already spent a night. The bungalow was in need of a complete refurb – every course to be raked out and repointed, new sashes – make that new window frames. The list wrote itself: replacement downspouts. A green, fan-shaped stain unfurled beneath a length of soffit . . . *and guttering.*

'That's a good slate roof you've up there, anyway. Uncommon for this area. Oxfordshire's mainly tile.'

'If you say so. Don't open it any further! What d'you think you're doing, Yori? If the hens get out this way, the dogs will have them.'

'Really?'

'*Really.*'

They edged into the poultry fustiness and he felt his eyes prickle. A violent sneeze threatened to knock him backwards against the door.

'Try not to scare the feathers off, can you? Winter's coming on.'

'I was thinking –'

'Open the far hatch. They'll go out themselves.'

'I could come back in a couple of months –'

'Well you've found your way here once.'

'– stay over for a while, maybe –'

'*Fully open*. Let them see the light.'

'– and do a few repairs.' The half-dozen tatty chickens formed up into a squad and made a break for the outside, yet another compartment, a fenced lawn of spent weeds and thin grass. Slamming the hatch down with force enough to threaten the hinges rewarded him with their squawks. He made for daylight himself, desperate for the yard, realizing he was holding his breath.

She was waiting, her expression sardonic. 'There's no cockerel now.'

'What happened?'

'The fox.'

'You have foxes here?'

'*Yori!* There are foxes everywhere. A vixen was in the lane last night, just before you got here – when I was looking out.'

'You were looking out?'

As they returned, they swished, the pair of them, though a drift of fallen leaves. They were litter from the shrub hard up against the kitchen wall, an elder whose roots beneath his tread he could feel strangling the drains. Any minute now, she reminded him, the *girls* would be dropped off. It was his turn to smile – *Yes, of course* – it being one of the things they'd talked about into the early hours. *No never lonely. Too busy – and of course there are the girls.* The girls that came from Didcot: Martha who just loved grooming Crook, the donkey – and Zadie or Maisie or whatever she was called, that was mad keen to walk the dogs. Was it imagination or could he hear the vehicle's drone already?

It would be jolting along the pitted track he'd cycled in the blackness, losing faith in his mother's directions.

'That's good Welsh slate up there,' he said again. 'A thirty degree pitch, probably copper-nailed. At least that's all right.'

# A CHRISTMAS BIRTHDAY

They were friends by an accident of geography. The village at the end of a long, narrow road to nowhere was without shop, church, pub or school but had over a hundred inhabitants scattered around its ancient green. To find six people – three couples – who got on and continued to get on for twenty years wasn't so unusual but they considered it lucky. They walked dogs, hacked out, had drinks in each others houses, went to films and plays and formed a clique to harass the council re 'green issues'. On Constance Smith's seventieth birthday the two younger couples, Bruce and Jackie Waller and David and Gwyneth Hughes, now in their fifties, had booked a table at Flaxfield.

It was a cold evening in December only days before Christmas when anything else takes effort to celebrate. Flaxfield, fifteen minutes away by car, offered a big decorated country house where other people were putting in all the work. Recently refurbished, under new management, according to local lore: ideal, they agreed. And they travelled in style. The Wallers' daughter, home from university, drove a bright yellow Volkswagon camper van, Daisy, a festival-going retro-rocket that would ferry them there and back. At eight o'clock Amy Waller had her father and Philip Smith wedged beside her in the front and the rest of the group arranged around a drop down table behind as though for a game of bridge. They set off along the only way out of the village, everyone but the chauffeur joining in the singing. The six were also the nucleus of the Christmas-only choir that carolled door to door for charity and something about the camper van interior had set them off. 'Deck the Halls', their best, was the natural starter followed by the 'Coventry Carol' which was a mistake and lowered the spirits. 'Ditch the carols,' came the plea from the front. 'We're All Going On A Summer Holiday' got them to the high road, a song too late for the Smith's teenage years and too early for the Hughes' and Wallers'. They knew it anyway. 'There was a film with it in – and . . . about a minibus,' someone suggested. 'Holidays in mini bus.'

'That doesn't seem quite right,' Gwyneth Hughes answered. The suggestion obviously had not been her husband's or she would have stopped at *Rubbish!*

'A red double-decker,' Philip Smith said.

'No-o!'

'A London bus.'

'Don't trust Philip,' his wife told them. 'He has no idea. And when he hasn't he makes things up.'

'True,' Philip Smith said and started on the verse about where the sun was shining brightly and the sky was blue and then gravel crunched under Daisy's wheels and they were there.

Flaxfield might have been imaged by Fizz. Its windows

blazed. They were unloaded under a tar black sky and umbrellas put up for a short walk from the carpark since freezing gusts carried rain. The Wirral poked between the estuaries of Mersey and Dee into the raging Irish Sea and was being battered from three directions.

'Behave now,' Amy Waller called after them. 'Ring when you want to be picked up.'

Inside – in the light and warmth – coats off, the women gave each other careful scrutiny. Jackie Waller, a small slim blonde had dressed for Christmas in shiny emerald satin which they all admired. 'Only Monsoon,' she said, 'in the summer sale.' Gwyneth Hughes, taller and dark, had stuck to her usual black. Constance Smith in blue cashmere looked best suited to a setting of hunting prints and ormolu and Victorian baubles. 'Very smart,' she was pronounced.

They made for the sofas drawn up to the fire, arriving just at the same time as a small florid man in pin-stripe trousers and waistcoat and a scarlet shirt. His mouth was already framing *can I get you –?* as Gwyneth Hughes launched into, 'Jackie met the last owner, you know. *The* Mrs Flaxney didn't you Jackie?'

'– anything to drink?' the man now seemed to butt in.

'Did you Jackie?' David Hughes teased her, 'Of course we all know you come from old money.'

'She was in her nineties – very frail. Quite sad really.'

Philip Smith wheezed and then put a quiver in his voice, 'Yes – we get like that, the elderly.' But he was running his hand through a head of luxuriant grey hair as he did it, looking like a poster boy for active retirement – as he knew.

'It was ages ago. I would take her the parish magazine, that's all. The drive was completely overgrown. You had to look out for potholes on your way around the back or you'd get soaked. That front door was never used.' She took in the huge room – and then up to a brace of chandeliers twenty feet above their heads. 'It must have needed a fortune spending on it . . . She used to have wild bird food delivered. Sacks of bird food every week. She'd been a racing driver, you know.'

They laughed at her. 'How are they connected?' David Hughes said.

'Well they're not, are they? I'm just –'

Bruce Waller interrupted, 'This chap's asking if we want something to drink.'

Gwyneth Hughes hardly looked at the waiter. Screwing up her eyes – a take-off of indecision for entertainment – she said, 'Oh I think that's very likely, don't you?' The tone wasn't meant. If it came out as dismissive, sarcastic, it wasn't meant.

Immediately all the males went into a huddle. Although Constance Smith's birthday, she didn't care for champagne Philip Smith reminded them, and it was just as well because had they seen the price of it? Further muttered negotiating and they were able to order a bottle of something with its twin for the ice bucket.

The waiter nodded, 'Well one's not gonna go far, is it?' in a strong local accent. Nobody responded.

On the other side of the fire Constance Smith, pale and pretty still at seventy, was telling the Wallers how she had spent the afternoon visiting family over in her native

Cheshire ... *Northwich* ... *Tarporley, back through Delamere Forest, too cold for a walk* – and she continued on. Gwyneth Hughes listened before turning to her own husband. 'That waiter's a bit – I mean, what he's dressed as? A snooker player ... or a –' she was going to add someone who works in a casino, not recalling the exact term, but David began a conversation with Philip Smith about a new wind turbine being developed by his university department (both men had trained in the sciences). Then Bruce Waller, who was in banking, described the financial crisis as reported by the lunchtime news – adding for Constance's benefit that *Cheshire would, of course, be immune* and then the wine arrived.

'Who's going to taste?' The waiter now had a white cloth over his arm and a bottle of Chardonnay and six glasses on a tray. These he transferred to the low table one at a time but with the last, Gwyneth's, he managed to insert his finger inside leaving a definite print. His brown hair, annoying close to her face in this operation, she decided was dyed.

'Just pour – that's fine,' Bruce Waller said.

Or perhaps a wig? 'I'll taste,' Gwyneth said, surprising them.

'Oo-o! Women's lib!' the waiter tried to involve others in jibe by looking around.

'But I'd like a clean glass.'

David Hughes raised his eyebrows. *Here we go*, they said.

The dining room was immense and mirrored to add bewildering perspectives – and only half-full. The second bottle had not made its appearance, though enquired after, before the waiter and a young woman in proper black and white arrived with food. She offloaded her plates and left. Then a bowl of soup was put down confidently in front of Gwyneth. Across the round table Constance Smith was looking at her delivery with distaste. Neither of them was able to get a word in. The waiter having caught Jackie Waller's eye was saying, 'I heard you talking about Mrs Flaxney. She was a right character, she was. 'Course I knew the family. It was all Liverpool money – so when she went, our firm had the winding up of the estate.'

'Really? I thought they were from –'

'I could *tell you* a few things about how the cash got made – I've been in the *legal* business, you know? You get to see what's at the back of it. All the skeletons in the cupboards. I'm meant to be retired but,' he gestured in the direction food had emerged from, 'they were desperate. So here I am.'

Gwyneth glared at Jackie who shrugged.

Only when he'd gone, 'Philip,' Constance Smith said, 'I didn't order this – does this smell of lemons to you?' They all knew she hated lemons, even their scent.

'It's my citrus watermelon,' Gwyneth said. 'If you're hoping for soup, Connie, I can help you out.' Gingerly they swapped. There was no bread. The men had begun eating anyway. 'What have you got there, Jackie?'

Jackie Waller prodded a speckled thing about the size of a ping-pong ball. Apart from a sprig of parsley, it was completely alone on a nine-inch dish. 'Um . . .'

'What's it meant to be?'

'Hazelnut dumpling.'

'You should send that back.'

Jackie said, 'Might be better than it looks.'

David said, 'It's Connie's birthday, Gwyn,' and managed to get a waitress serving another table over to say they'd need that wine *now* please.

They drank to Constance.

'To Connie!'

'Happy Birthday and many of them!'

'Well this is very nice,' Philip Smith said, looking around.

The Christmas tree's lights were visible behind him. They were the type that winked on and off in sequence and kept attracting her attention whenever Gwyneth looked his way. All around everything that stuck out from anything else had been gilded. If it was flat it had been marbled. The carpet was woven with a curlicue motif that could just be deciphered as an italic *F*. The walls were papered in the colour of the waiter's shirt. And he was back, trying to clear too soon. There was not much else to take exception to, apart from the shrieks of a big all-female party at the other end of the room. Gwyneth was noticed to be watching them by Jackie. 'I'm sure they're teachers,' she told her friend because Jackie Waller was an ex-teacher herself. 'Knocking it back – all that shouting, they couldn't be anything else.'

Jackie gave up on the dumpling and sipped her drink. 'Poor things,' she said complacently.

So Gwyneth leaned in across her husband and hissed at her, 'The food's dreadful.'

'I know. We should really – but –'

But the Smiths had eaten theirs, probably out of politeness, and were now listening to Bruce Waller's telling them what a parcel of grazing had just gone for at auction. His wife and Gwyneth had bought their first horse between them twenty-five years ago. Once the number of beasts had risen to six, now it was down again to two but horses – their temperaments, fitness, ailments and feeding regimes – were a constant topic among the group, with dogs and cats a close second. 'Poor drainage, no shelter – if you did some work, it's still only suitable, say, for a couple of Shetlands –'

'I'll bet you didn't know,' the waiter said putting Constance Smith's chicken in front of him, 'that Dick Turpin came here.'

'No. Mine's the Dover sole. Thank you. *So* what we're getting is a third market, half way between agricultural prices and development land –'

'He was the highwayman. You know? Been tried and sentenced to *hang* – then he escaped and him and Black Bess swum the *Mersey*,' the waiter's voice increased in volume so that at *Mersey* they and everybody else in the room were forced to look at him. 'And *then* just when he gets all that way to the Wirral side, the horse drops dead – right out there, it was. Right in front. You won't find that in the books.'

Jackie giggled but softly; researching local history was another of their joint interests. Gwyneth couldn't help but say, 'I don't think so. That's William Massey you're mixing him up with. Local aristo. Coming back from the Battle of Preston – where he'd been on the losing side – he swam his horse across the river. It fell dead in the courtyard of *Puddington* Hall.'

The man's mobile mouth became a fixed line in his face.

It was an odd face – and not quite the same one, Gwyneth realised, that had served their drinks. Still ruddy and round, the eyes in it were very deep-set and shadowed, while her inattention had filled them in as normal or even protrusive. She put it down to refusing to wear her glasses when she came out in the evening. Her *entré* landed with a thud, then the one next to her, her husband's. David's hand groped for and squeezed her knee beneath the tablecloth. 'That's torn it,' he said looking into a bowl of bouillabaisse that was still in motion. Something's shell poked above its surface; the rest was muddy as the Mersey. 'I won't be getting my bread now.'

Her risotto was chalky.

Trying to discount what they ate, they chatted about the prospect of the village's ancient drainage system being defeated by the downpour and then how much they were all paying for heating oil – and the Wallers' chances of getting Christmas cards now that Elvis had bitten the postman. 'I hope we don't,' Jackie said, 'because I can never get round to putting them up.' But a doubling of fuel prices, the fields' runoff lapping at their thresholds or a summons from Royal Mail were paper tigers. A dependable farm worker would unblock the drains. They owned woodland and could burn logs *come the great collapse*, Bruce suggested. If necessary Elvis would be provided with the best defence money could buy. The result would be his acquittal.

'He'll be bound over to keep the peace,' David said.

'Oh no. Asbo'd!' Jackie countered.

'On the subject of keeping the peace . . .' Philip Smith gestured with a nod. On their raucous way back to the lounge the teachers' party were approaching. One unsteady member of it, spaghetti straps at half-mast, almost rested on Philip's knee as she passed.

'Will that be the headmistress, do we think?' he murmured after a moment's pause. He was a courteous man who wouldn't dream of allowing a drunken woman to know herself ridiculed.

'Head,' Jackie corrected. 'You have to leave out the mistress now. Yes – it probably is.'

Three or four couples remaining soon followed them out although it wasn't yet ten. The birthday party, last to be seated, were alone. 'We can sing it, now,' David suggested and they did.

'I'm not sure what we're celebrating,' Constance said.

'Oh-h, we should have ordered a cake,' David said.

'No you shouldn't.'

'He's only wanting one himself,' Bruce Waller said.

'Think what it would be like from here!' Gwyneth had to go and say – and got a nudge.

The waiter had come up on them during 'Happy Birthday'. He removed first Constance Smith's chicken, not giving her time to ask for it to be wrapped for the cat. 'Last week it was murder,' he said.

Someone said 'Oh?' but Gwyneth couldn't decide who it was to kick. 'Anything else?' she asked the table. 'Connie? I'm –'

'Now – you'll want to hear this,' the waiter said. 'Just

outside the bar – that way, it is – I come across this guest, well I say guest, as you'll see *not*, and he's on his phone and he's going something like *I'll just get this done – no I don't know how long it'll take, do I?* and as he turns I see he's got a gun in his pocket. A real gun. I kid you not!'

Gwyneth and Jackie exchanged a look and Jackie shook her head. But Gwyneth said, 'Can we see the dessert menu?'

'So what do I do? I put the drinks down, just casual and I go like I'm walking past – I've done some acting so it's easy enough. I tackle him don't I? And he's off his guard. He's up against the wall and I've got hold of the gun before he knows what's hit him.'

'You've got a spot of something on your dress Jackie, just on the right – no, my right.'

'I can't see it.'

'*It turns out* he was the murderer! It was Pink Panther Night. He's a stunt man they get over from Manchester.'

'And they hadn't told you! Gosh. So that makes you really brave! Except it wasn't a real gun.' Only Philip Smith laughed with her. 'I can still see it Jackie – you've made it worse now. So – who's for the Flaxfield Special Fondant? I am!'

'Chocolate sponge and cheesecake both off,' the waiter said. He didn't appear sorry. The bruised stare became glassy as his mind turned inward – and he was puffing now as though fresh from a fight. And very red. In other circumstances he might have seemed dangerous, especially when he exhaled into her face and Gwyneth smelled brandy. But her friends were ranged in a circle around her, the lights behind Philip twinkled idiotically – and she must have drunk too much because she snapped, 'What's *not off,* then?'

'Christmas pudding.'

'That's it?' Bruce Waller joined in.

'We-ll, it's a tough choice but it looks like . . . Christmas pudding for six,' Philip Smith attempted.

'This is a birthday party for God's sake!'

'It's all right. We like Christmas pudding. We've been *hoping* for Christmas pudding, Connie and I –'

Gwyneth said, 'Can't chef do something lighter? Meringues? Jackie – wouldn't you like that?'

'Mm – yes.'

The waiter added disgust to the repertoire of his face. As he turned and strutted off Gwyneth saw that some time during the evening he had rolled up the sleeves of the scarlet shirt to show muscular, grey-fuzzed forearms, not a lawyer's arms, whatever a lawyer's arms were like . . . nor an actor's – perhaps they were stripped in readiness for washing-up. Guilt seeped into her and self-reproach. What was she doing on Connie's birthday, Connie who was sitting across from her, smiling politely at Bruce Waller's optimistic house-price forecast, not really minding what people talked about nor the lack of choice on the menu? But the man was having a peculiar effect: present he made her combative and – she admitted it now – wanting to humiliate. As soon as he disappeared she was sorry, reminding herself that the kitchen's shortcomings were not his – and that she was very definitely not from money old or new.

Four Christmas puddings came quickly via the girl.

David Hughes said, 'I've got to eat this?'

'Yes,' Gwyneth said. 'You didn't back me up over the meringues.'

Philip Smith chewed on his first mouthful and said, 'D'you get the impression our man doesn't want us to think he's only a waiter?'

'Only *just* a waiter,' Bruce Waller said.

There followed a delay long enough to notice Flaxfield gone quiet around them. The Smiths smiled at each other. Jackie rubbed at the spot on her dress. David repeated, 'Well, happy birthday again, Connie,' and clinked his glass against hers.

The heavy curtains, tied up in numerous ruches and gathers, gave glimpses of a garden in the seeping light. Gwyneth imagined it as perfect in daytime: simpler and older than the present house, its cobbles and stone and clipped box hedges the enduring bone structure of a *grand dame*. Mrs Flaxney came into her head and she was about to ask Jackie whether there was a portrait or photograph anywhere when, in the distance, a noise half way between a bang and a clatter made them both jump.

'Chef's just banjoed Jeeves,' David Hughes offered.

Bruce Waller pointed to his untouched plate. 'Chef's long gone.'

And – if there were no portrait – what had been hinted at just now? Did the man mean . . . was he trying to say here was another case of Liverpool slavers? *The Trade* as it was once called, needing no other explanation as the making of so many fortunes according to Wirral legend, the Tarletons, the Gregsons, the Leylands – perhaps even the Earle's whose name was given to the green lane her own house stood on. Was that it – the Flaxneys tainted also? She'd found no hint in her researches . . . which had been pretty amateurish or so they seemed now. But, *'Dick Turpin!'* she mocked and David tapped his temples with a finger, Connie squeezed her eyes shut in mock despair, Bruce said, 'Got to be the truth, hasn't it?' Their table turned mournful. Things they were already rehearsing, coffee around the fire, the exchange of fresh gossip and familiar stories, the jokes about Philip's thriftiness, David's sweet tooth, Bruce's receding hairline, became dubious. And more was at stake: the wait for Amy's entrance in her multi-coloured jacket, giant boots, silver charms rattling in her dreadlocks. The comfortable ritual they'd collude in as her mother said, 'Oh Amy!' and her father muttered, 'Just look!' but in pride. And if other guests did look as she marched to join them, all the better. Making room, six becoming seven, it would be a perfect winding down – before, louder and more care-less, they were formally helped into coats and then piled into Daisy. Rowdier than teachers, one of them would say. If they could be observed by the hotel manager and Christmas residents, better still.

Gwyneth finished her glass, filched and knocked back her husband's wine, and felt fury bloom with the double hit. 'Where's that bloody man got to?' she hissed so that, she believed, only David and Jackie could hear.

'Two meringues!'

The waiter's hand came into her peripheral vision at the instant Gwyneth heard it. Sober she might have jumped. Jackie's plate was down and the man turned on his heel before Gwyneth said, 'What? Wait. Excuse me! Could you come back please?'

He did stop. After a count of five, maybe.

'Is this it?'

A dry meringue rosette, the size of a cup cake and off-white against the plate's glaze, had been put in front of her. Jackie's was similar though slightly less knocked about.

'You can't be serious.'

The man's face filled out into one more incarnation: toad. Gwyneth thought his wide smirk almost predatory. 'Meringues,' he said spreading the second syllable lovingly and, his hand just hovering over Jackie's plate, he snatched Gwyneth's pudding – parapudding she might have christened it given time – crumbled it onto one big flat palm then threw it like wedding rice over the table. It fell on Philip Smith's half-raised spoon, into the glass of port the waitress had brought for Bruce Waller and speckled David Hughes' charcoal jacket.

'Oh, I say,' Constance Smith protested. She had spoken least the whole evening. Now it was the rest of them stayed dumb.

Having seen what could be achieved, the man grabbed Jackie's meringue before anyone at the table could believe he would, pulverised it in both hands this time achieving finer aggregate, and threw it at them all in turn. The young woman engaged in setting up for breakfast in the room's furthest corner, came over, met Gwyneth's eyes and hurried in the direction of the kitchen. Still the waiter waited, his arms dropped to his sides. Having the audience he craved seemed to have the effect of a sudden corpsing.

'Well,' came from Philip Smith.

'Just leave it,' Bruce Waller said when Jackie turned expectantly to him.

David Hughes attempted to stifle a cough but the sight of his wife, flakes hanging from her dark fringe made him snort with laughter. Gwyneth transferred her anger to him temporarily, driving his amusement beyond control.

Bruce Waller got up from the table saying, 'I'll call Amy,' as another, younger man arrived. Tall, olive skinned and black-haired he inclined over the debris steadying himself on the back of Constance's chair. His style was also inno-vatory – an immaculate tawny suit, lemon shirt and soft peach tie. But when he spoke – 'Ah – I see,' – his accent was pure to the point of archaism, very BBC World Service to Gwyneth's ear.

'Good evening,' the newcomer said. 'I'm Yagoub Sorush, the manager. There's a problem, yes? Thank you, Des – I'll take care of this table now.' While the waitress brushed the meringue bits into a small wooden receptacle, he straight-ened the unused cutlery, noticed wine in the bottle and topped up the nearest (Constance's) glass. A moment passed while everyone held their collective breath. The waiter left. They listened to his brisk march across the parquet until Gwyneth said, 'He's gone.'

'I'm sorry about this.'

'Yes,' Philip said, 'not quite what you'd expect.'

'No – no. Of course not. May I get you –' His grimace revealed bleached teeth, his expression baffled but closing on exasperation. '– it's difficult, you see, and quite sad . . . actually. I am extremely sorry.' Adding, oddly, 'Flaxfield is sorry,' he opened his hands to display them. They were accepting the shame. 'Let me get you something to finish off – as my guest. More to drink? Liqueurs, perhaps?' You could see him stiffen at sudden steps behind his back but it was Bruce Waller returned to announce Amy was on her way.

'I think I'd like to go – unless anyone else . . . ?' Constance Smith's voice was almost a whisper but had them all on their feet.

'Just the bill,' Bruce Waller said as David Hughes said, 'The bill please,' at the same time.

Yagoub Sorush made a gesture with his handsome head. 'We will of course not charge for dessert – and would deducting the cost of the wine be acceptable, yes? Please allow me to.'

While they lingered in the hall – it seemed to take an age recovering Philip Smith's Burberry – Jackie found quite a large piece of meringue in Gwyneth's ear and held it up for her to see. It was tenacious stuff. As Gwyneth helped Constance into her coat she heard the crunch of it down one sleeve of the blue cashmere. A grandfather clock struck the half hour. The men stood muttering. Constance smiled brightly and gave one of her quick schoolgirlish shoulder movements – at the excitement of it all. Lights went out in the dining room beyond the glass doors and Yagoub Sorush offered his final goodnight, his final *so sorry* before moving smoothly out of sight. The young woman wished them all a Merry Christmas. A smart couple, residents – she stick-thin, his paunch well-tailored – were the last to come from the direction of the lounge. They began a slow ascent of the staircase without speaking. Each of the friends felt varying degrees of embarrassment and recognised it in one another. There would be a time in their collective future where *that dinner, that waiter* would begin an enjoyable round of talk. Details would be picked out, the loudness and the tipsiness of the teachers exaggerated. The spot on Jackie's dress would grow, the meringueing of Gwyneth's hair become slapstick – but for now Gwyneth felt that if they all were still here when the clock struck the quarter hour, she would scream.

Amy appeared in the porch. They called out greetings that sounded flat and false even to their own ears and answered *Yes!* and *Pretty good!* to her question about the evening. But no one was inclined to start on a story of his or her own, no *You won't believe what happened with* . . . The rain at least had stopped and the sky cleared and once Daisy was off the high road, the winter constellations could be picked out over the invisible fields. Singing didn't happen. Constance thanked them again for treating her and they shrugged or said *oh well* or *no need for thanks* with a tinge of something that passed Amy by. And as Daisy lurched around familiar bends in the lane, braked for a cat or maybe a rabbit, Gwyneth was debating *why couldn't I just listen to him? My father was a waiter, once. Why not just listen?*

# A GIRL'S ARM

Norway suits me – and this town of Alesund and this life.
I've made mistakes. But that's the beauty of it. You can start
again here, fresh as a five-year-old at the school gate. The
past doesn't have come top. Alesund is a prime example
of that. More than a century ago – in Jan 1904 – it actually burned to the ground. Being a port, but with the whole
thing made of wood and clustered tight up and squeezed
onto a narrow strip of land, it wasn't hard. Ten thousand
made homeless overnight – there are pictures of the aftermath on show everywhere, almost defiantly, because, well,
just see it now. That's what Alesundians should say. *Se oss
na!* I do. I love it every day. Because after the fire, architects
came from all over Europe and made a new painted town
of plaster friezes and curved ironwork and door handles
shaped like leaves. *Se oss na!* Perhaps it takes an outsider
to appreciate what the natives miss.

I was born by the sea but a different sea. I come from the
sort of Welsh village that can only look good on a postcard.
Cottages owned by English weekenders front a harbour for
their boats. We're not talking Cowes here, but one rubble
jetty and two cross pontoons. The dinghies and cabin cruis-
ers hardly move from where the fishing fleet once went out

every day. Merlyn's Rock guards the only channel in, on it the stump of a tower put up by Lord Somebody or Other over a couple of summers and swept away in 1932 by a single storm. Every year the rounded hump of the foundation is scoured that bit smoother so local kids can get away with calling it Merlyn's Ball. The stone in this part of Wales is a cold grey when not black-wet, but with the cottages done up and all the pleasure crafts at their moorings, the sun can give a lift to the area around the inlet. Occasionally a sightseeing tour out of Chester or Liverpool will think it worth a swing by. To the west up against a green hill stands the Conway Hotel, 'the monstrosity'. Four storeys of brick soak up the light even in good weather, as does the massive roof, steep as a ski slope. But it has views out to sea and along the entire length of Ferry Lane that follows the shoreline. From the Conway you can watch the progress of the few day trippers that find their way down from the main road. After ice cream, a stroll around takes all of five minutes. Time for a drink at the Puffin Inn that was once run by the famous Abel Jones. (He had been a smuggler and bare-knuckle fighter.) Or facing a strip of shingle there's a takeaway that sells rubber chicken – and a wall and a flower bed to eat it off and throw rubbish into. Further on the social club is in the shape of an American ranch house to serve the campsite behind, then a Londis store and the pay and display. Holiday spirit comes to a halt with the Bar. This is where huge slabs cut off the cliffs at the eastern end of the bay are loaded onto barges. Everything is dreary with dust including the road and bushes meant to screen the portakabins, the mess and the motorised belt. When the wind blows from this direction the whole village turns into Pompeii.

That view from the third floor of the Conway – in fact from the grubby sash window on the far right – is still picture perfect because it's the one I grew up with. I saw it every day, high season and low, for years. My mother and I arrived with me barely able to walk. We occupied Room 202 – the Manx Suite in the hotel's heyday but by 1979 when we moved in, a flat. The Conway had become housing. Hostel would be more accurate.

Michelle was the daughter of a newsagent and his wife whose shop off Ferry Lane – at the quarrying end – had accommodation over it. All three managed there pretty well apparently, until I came along. So my grandmother said. Vic and Audrey were not pleased to be made grandparents when they had hardly reached forty themselves. And then above the shop wasn't spacious. After months of sniping – Grandad Vic I hardly remember apart from his cough and nicotine smell, but Audrey was definitely the sniping kind – Michelle took herself off with me in her arms and presented us to the local council as homeless. 202, The Conway was their remedy. A huge room had been split into living, sleeping and kitchen cubicles and then barely furnished. Only the living section kept its plaster ceiling with the cherubs so when Granny Audrey visited she and my mother had to sit under a riot of the sort of things that had caused all the trouble. There was a bathroom but you needed to go out onto the landing to get to it. Annoying when you are living with a small boy and a bedwetter but to be fair to my mother she didn't make a fuss. She was one

of those pink, round faced, soft bodied sort of Welsh girls
that never run, never knock things over, never raise their
voices especially to a child. They stare at you a long time
with their blue eyes before saying anything at all. (Audrey
to my mother, more than once, said 'You should've been a
damn sight quicker saying no!')

We lived side by side with other single mothers and
babies plus older, twitchy couples who had lost homes
according to Audrey through debt and complained about
noise – and solitary young males. These often had some
defect for a boy to pick up on, a limp or terrible acne scars
or a way of hunching the body as though it was a massive
effort to climb the Conway's ten cracked steps. I remember one of them – his name was Wes, I'm sure it was Wes,
gangly *and* spotty – he kept his left hand in his jacket pocket
all the time. All the time he talked to me on the wall waiting
for Michelle to come down and let me in – he was usually
about – and all the time we played football on the coarse
grass. I tortured myself over what was held in that hand. Or
was it so deformed and horrible nobody could be allowed
to see? A scaly claw like a heron's, say, or covered in sores?
Did I really want to know – or not?

But then a child went missing that last year, a visitor's
child, and people said there must have been some accident,
anyway the child turned up next day, drowned. Michelle
got careful after that. I never saw Wes's hand.

Vic died. Audrey hung on in the newsagents, alone and
mad for a while and then invited us back. Not a change
for the better – gone was my gull's eye view of the weekenders arriving in cars I recognised with wives and dogs

I could match to The Loft and *Oystercatcher* or Bay Vista and *Speedy Soo II*. Even the fat old ladies heaving themselves off the coach in coats because only when they made it to the seats would the coloured dresses come on show, I missed them too. What I regretted most were the families that materialised from the tents. The first day, before they were as bored with the place as the rest of us, you could see them decide to just chill together on the shingle. Windbreaks going up, tartan rugs out, the man would be off to the water straightaway. Stones would be thrown if there were boys and, mentally, I'd be down there with them. My stone would be further out than all the others. My stone would do six, seven, eight skips so that the dad shouted Wow! Oh Wow! Look at it go! Fan-tastic! You could hear it from the Conway, he'd be so impressed.

The woman and daughters stay nearer their belongings, food in airtight boxes being laid on a rug as if on a table, towels unpacked, a yellow Frisby, the turquoise lilo – and then the girls come wriggling out of their clothes too quick for Mum! The shorts and top and knickers are off and she still hasn't found the bathers.

In Alesund, though, everything was fine, or mainly fine, until Janikka, my wife, surprised me asking about my father. Her expression was nice and her glossy lips were nearly in the smile with the two symmetric dimples. She has light brown hair caught in a band, pulled back for work but she could never look severe, not Janikka. The hair was only just fixed and already bits have escaped, curling around her ears and getting into her top button. We were sitting across the table from one another, the coffee drunk but with its scent still hanging around and her bag next to her, zipped up saying she would be out the door any second. Her job is at the tourist information point on Skansegata. Hoards straight off the cruise ships are all anxious to see Alesund, the rebuilt town and Janikka behind her counter is their first stop. If I saw her, I'd drop in.

She didn't need to be there until ten but it was quarter to – and she came out with, 'Why Geraint do you not talk to me about your father?'

She said my name *Gerr-aint-e* but this was no time to correct it. Married for nearly a year, I hoped we'd dealt with all the usual stuff, Welsh childhood, single mother, no real need for details – however she was just back from one of her trips down to Bergen to meet The Hag. I should have been prepared for something. Solveig Heggestad is her twin. As unlike Janikka as a distant cousin, she is older by an hour and likes to play the big sister and the big success. She teaches at the University. She lives with Per Sunde, a famous journalist – in Norway – who guests on NRK discussion programmes and writes books about what's wrong with his country. Janikka worships Solveig. And Solveig has never liked me.

Janikka smiled now properly, stood and gave her skirt a pull down over the curve of both hips. The sun was just getting into the apartment and she looked attractive but not unapproachable, standing there on well-muscled legs tanned darker than the tights. Her white blouse showed a hint of strain across big breasts. I could imagine the men, the foreigners who are always trying to pick her up, thinking she's typical Norwegian, the fantasy in a navy suit. She is thirty-five soon, older than me but she believes she is younger. This is not a criticism, not a Granny Audrey snipe, but fact. She believes it because that's what I've told her – just as she believes my name is Geraint Johns.

I made a thing of gathering up cups, plates and a sticky glass while I concocted my answer. But the moment and its danger passed. Janikka laughed. 'Oh, now you are funny face. Solveig says all man –'

'Men,' I said reflexively.

'*Tak.* All men become the fathers so I must ask you about your father soon.'

We have no clock in the kitchen, just a pair of giant aluminium hands on the wall with a secret mechanism that is hell to get to and change the battery. I looked at it now.

Janikka said, 'OK! See you later.' I got a mint-smelling kiss on the forehead since she's a fraction taller than me and I was in bare feet. First the bag then the coat were grabbed on her way out and the click of heels faded on the other side of the door. If I wandered over to the front of the apartment I could watch her swivel left, taking the green route to work around the edge of the park. But today I didn't. My pulse was racing, the cream from the coffee rancid in my mouth. I drank water and splashed some on my face. A mirror was something else we didn't have in the kitchen which was just as well. As a non-shaver whose hair and beard is clipped by a barber on Kirkegata every month, a look at myself's the last thing I ever wanted. With Solveig's challenge still pumping me up, I opened the laptop on the breakfast bar and got down to the latest patter received overnight. An owner of some fishing cabins on the island of Giske was trying to hook me. Next week maybe, I send back, I'll come see. My business – trollands.com – is a bespoke travel service for Norway, specialising in the less accessible top half of the country. Basically from here in Alesund, which is not that far north though you can feel the Pole's breath on your neck, and all the way up to Tromsø above the Arctic Circle, if you want to do the independent thing but with the annoying details sorted, I am your man. My reputation is excellent in the industry and deserves to be. I can put together a complicated but seamless itinerary in record time. In the recent volcanic ash no-fly emergency – when you didn't need a word of Norwegian to translate the headline *Vulkan Aske fra Island* STOPPED FLY-NORGE – I returned an entire German sales team to their office by cargo freighter with the loss of just a single day's wine-merchanting. Give me some warning, though, and I'll over-please. A bachelor party from the City of London? My kayaking special, coupled with nights of outdoor dancing and pickups on Sandsøya, will make the honeymoon an anticlimax. If you are the six Pettersens from Grand Forks, Minnesota of massive waistlines and Norwegian descent, I'll get you into the settlement on the Trondheimsfjord your ancestors escaped from, get you a schematic of the graveyard, and get you out again without missing a meal. I've just done it. An email from Herkie Pettersen was here to tell me how well I had, with a couple of pictures attached for my website. The Pettersens would need to be a lot less broad and ugly to be of any use. Their gushing recommendations, perhaps – but it was no good. More routine matters and bookings I sent on to my assistant, Erik. He's a housebound ex-teacher on the outskirts of Alesund. We've never met.

4 u eric.

Because thanks to Solveig, I couldn't work.

Outside it was mid-May. Soon there'd be blossom in the park but I picked up a sweater with my keys. We live at street level on Radstugata which is an expensive address and the apartment is tiny and we just stretch to it. There's even a reminder of Wales to the left of our building, the Metodistkirken, which would please my Granny Audrey if she weren't safely tucked up in a home and had any idea where and who I was now. In front, with its play area and Japanese cherries still in waiting, is a rising grassy open space. It's already occupied by a stream of American silver-surfers or Germans or British, they're becoming harder to sort, on their collective way to the foot of The Fjellstua's 418 steps. The lookout – from here they will get the whole of reincarnated Alesund and its quayside and piers, ferries zipping over to the looming islands and – on a day like today – the brilliant blue Atlantic and distant glint off the Sunnmøre peaks. Ships at anchor are sized for the bathtub, speedboats are albino tadpoles. *Tideekpress*, the catamaran to Haried, is a working model for some lucky kid. Ginger and red and white buildings are steep-roofed like doll's houses with green foam for trees separating the streets.

All this they'll take in for an average of seven and a half minutes according to tourist board research. Then they'll hobble down again.

A watery sun came out that wouldn't set until half past ten. When people talk about Norway that old myth about the long nights is what you hear first. Drives you to alcoholism, they say – to suicide. My bet is on the endless days for sending you over the edge. Too many hours to watch and think are dangerous – but it's a myth anyway, about the Norwegians. In comparison to the Welsh, they're wild optimists. They're Vikings, their national motto is 'Plan – what Plan?' Look how they smoke! They expect to live forever. I met Janikka, my future wife when I was not exactly suicidal but down in one of life's dips, my third and worst of them. It was she who gave me a hand up.

The first dip lasted for the years I had to waste back at the newsagent's shop – thanks to Audrey. Under her regime again, she managed to creep in and get between me and my mother. She knew better than a full frontal attack now – it was what had sent us to the Conway. Instead she chipped away, like one of those machines chewing at the cliffs at the far end, making Trebor Bay a bit bigger and a lot murkier every year.

'If it was just the two of us we could go on a nice trip. There's one here in the paper – cheap. You go to Amsterdam on the coach and then see the tulip fields. I'd love to see the tulip fields.'

'Too much for him,' Michelle said. She'd be trying to do the shop accounts. I think I get my attention to detail from my mother. 'He'd never be still all that time, not on a bus.'

'Vic always promised me we'd go when he retired.'

'It isn't the sort of holiday for a child, though, is it?'

'No – well.' Though pale as Michelle's, Audrey's face was nothing like my mother's. It was heavier, almost mannish, especially as she aged – and turned on me it was always toxic. There was something about my oily dark hair and skinnyness, probably, something she couldn't get over.

'Perhaps when he's older?'

'Huh! I don't suppose I'll ever get to see the tulips now.'

The year after I started secondary school Ted, the campsite owner, began his campaign. We were on his route. We sold the *Daily Express*. At first my mother would have nothing to do with him. 'Old enough to be my dad!' (Audrey, 'You could do a lot worse, our Michelle. In fact you have done. He's steady – he thinks the world of you.') Gradually he wore her down. He dressed in Levis and cowboy boots with fake spurs but he watched her like he was her pet dog. I could see a drink at the Puffin with Ted was better than an evening in. I had nothing against Ted because he played the guitar and sang on Country and Western nights at the campsite and I imagined him coming to pick up Michelle one time and for some reason he'd have his guitar with him and suggest I could learn. Then we'd find I was brilliant at it, hardly needing lessons. Girls, particularly Brianne Wallis, would start hanging round when I went to the Music Room at dinnertimes and Mrs Hamner, the music teacher, would be going *Amazing! Such natural talent!* It never happened. Once the Puffin got to be a regular thing, Ted stopped noticing me. And my worries grew that one day Michelle would move in with him and I'd be left alone with Audrey like old stock.

Audrey didn't trust me unsupervised down in the shop and she was right not to. Living above a cigarette mine meant this dark skinny kid could at least stave off suffering at school. Apart from Darrell Pugh I had no friends and with Darrell it was only how he was team captain of everything and I was a reasonable second striker – fast. The newsagent's wasn't the sort of place your mates called round, drank free Tangos and you all went off to the Youth Club. It had a handwritten sign stuck inside the door ONLY TWO PUPILS FROM CENNARD HIGH AT A TIME INSIDE. Cennard High was my school.

Thieving was a stressful trade and I lived on my nerves never sure which was worst, Audrey or the 5D smokers. But I came out alive and with a brain honed to operate in any available market. I left. *Passes in both Maths and English,* my report read, *a good all-rounder* – it was the most positive comment anyone had ever made about me. I went to work for Watkins and Nurse, the estate agents. Lettings, though, became my specialty and a year later, freedom came with the move to head office in Llandudno Junction and a room in one of their client's houses. I was on the way up. The night I sat on my bed, my belongings still unpacked, the stain on the ceiling telling me it would become an old friend and the voices from the street seeping through the failed double glazing, I felt full of energy and a spark of something else. It was unfamiliar but good and was probably hope.

Which is how these kids, boys of fifteen, sixteen maybe, look to me now. I'm sitting outside the Hoffmann Garden, my favourite café, in the sun with a Coke and on the next table there they are suddenly. Red-faced, all in new naval uniforms, their money in notes and coins being counted out – Janikka had mentioned there was a training ship in the harbour from Tallinn, a three-master. The cadets consult the menu, take shifty looks at me, then exchange a lot of Estonian – on the subject of cost it doesn't take a genius to work out. I catch the eye of good old Dagrun through the glass, hold up my Coke and four fingers. Even as I do it, I know it's a mistake. But Dagrun, who wouldn't come straight out for anyone who wasn't a reliable customer, brings them their drinks. With a disapproving pout she drops off my bill which I detain her to pay. After the confusion among the sailors, the tallest, reddest faced one is sent over with a few words. I try to appear bored. On the edge of my vision I see him salute and hear the rest of his gang hoot with either encouragement or mockery. A mistake, I repeat in my head. Now I have to leave when I'd meant to linger till twelve, treat myself to lunch, maybe. Wait as Kongensgata gradually livens up and the sun picks out the plasterwork trees on the building directly opposite.

My second bad patch came when I was just into my twenties. On behalf of Watkins and Nurse I set out with the keys to a holiday cottage in the back of beyond – it was on a sheep farm inland. Usually it would be let only three or four months of the year if we were lucky. This was a raw spring morning and the farm was nearly impossible to find. When I did, I was directed down the hill again to a stone building I'd mistaken for a tractor shed with the owner's suggestion of, 'And if the bugger's still there tell 'im he's got today to get gone.' The tenant had taken a six-month lease after the season was over but had now overstayed. It was my job to recover payment and gain repossession.

I approached Cosy Cot's only door trying to keep my shoes cleanish – and a rat shot out of the black rubbish bag on the step and just missed my feet. I knocked. Nothing. I stood back. No smoke from the chimney. A circuit of the building showed every curtain was closed. At least one big key on the bunch fitted and turned – it was not unknown for locks to have been changed in this sort of situation – and I called out my name and business before stepping inside. The air was freezing but also rank. Though it had never happened to me so far, you can always get in a funk over what you're going to find. I flicked the light switch and breathed again – the room was vacant. A sofa against the far wall was draped with items of men's clothing and some magazines. A couple of armchairs were aimed at an empty grate so choked with ash it spilled out onto the bare wooden boards and stirred in the draught from the door. But the coffee table was the worst thing. The top was invisible under mugs and glasses and polystyrene trays – it was out of one of these a gobbet of mould sprouted like a dead squirrel's tail.

'Fucking great!' I said aloud. Just to be on the safe side I called my name out again but the only sound anywhere was from the farm cockerel up the hill. Leaving the door open behind me I edged past the rot holding my breath and went through into a tiny kitchen. Not as bad as it could have been. A ketchup bottle was welded to the draining board by its own run-off, the sink was full of more mugs, brown inside but dry. The weirdest thing was what must have been well over a hundred empty cans of cider, laid on their sides and stacked to form a perfect pyramid on the

Formica top. Their poked out eyes faced forward. A hint of apples lingered in their corner.

Of course I knew what I was doing. There were still two closed doors, a bathroom off the kitchen and the bedroom next to it. An old hand at Watkins and Nurse had felt he ought to set me right when I'd moved into lettings. 'Now your bathrooms are your prime locations for doing-away-withs, bedrooms for natural causes.'

Cosy Cot's shower room was foul as feet but also too tight for ending it all.

At the last closed door like a fool I had to go and knock. The dirty bulb came on to show a double divan, unmade, a greasy grey pillow on the floor, a cupboard hanging open and nothing inside. Bits and pieces, a disposable lighter, coppers, cigarette papers, lay on top of an old-fashioned dressing table. I had already got out the mobile to see if I could find a signal and order up the cleaning crew – that was the deal we had with the owner, for cleaning and main-tenance – when something made me go across and open a drawer. A plastic wallet was in the bottom, the sort of thing you might keep car details in. This one though bulged with extras, printed papers, envelopes, handwritten stuff.

The thought of sitting on that damp bed was gross. I clicked off the light and went back to the open air and stood, braced against a windowsill and out of the wind, to take my first look.

It was somebody's life. A first quick rifle through was enough to tell me that, everything being in the same name. Letters, envelopes, most of them the brown ones with plastic windows, plus more official things, like our expired lease, were pushed in with scruffy notes on lined paper, bills and receipts and oddities like a demand from Denbighshire libraries for the return of the half dozen books listed and with current fines owed of £14.60p. It was dated over a year ago.

A lot of what has happened – including me, here now this day in Alesund – happened because of that decision made outside Cosy Cot. And yet I can't remember how long it took me, or why I did it – or even why I bothered to waste time over the missing tenant's paper trail while freezing my buttocks on a stone sill and with some sort of hawk screaming overhead like on Discovery Channel. Take it back to the office, common sense will have told me. Hand it over to Cuddy Cuthbertson – the retired credit controller who did this sort of work for beer money. But I carried on looking.

A quick flick – and there was a path through the chaos with a direction that didn't need signposting. The red electricity bill for an address down the coast, not one of ours, came before the library's demand. Then more scribblings were followed by an official whinge about a missed appointment at somewhere called the Berwyn-May Clinic. This was dated only the previous month and was the last piece of correspondence. Till receipts from a garage were for food items – and from Bargain Booze for all those cans. A thick block of handwritten stuff came after, like a diary but without dates. Finally – I almost missed it, tucked into an NHS booklet on healthy eating – was the maroon passport.

Although everything that had passed through my hands

referred to an individual called Geraint Johns, none of it
made much of an impact on me until I opened the passport. I was a smart twenty-two and I'd entered abandoned
properties regularly by this time and become pretty cool,
so I believed, about people's leavings. Kitchens alive with
maggots and more than one homicidal cat had greeted
me. A passport was unusual – worth something, probably.
But I opened it with only low-grade curiosity for a sight of
whoever was going to be costing Watkins and Nurse and
Farmer Davies up the road some hard cash.

What I found myself staring at was – my own face.

I don't mean Geraint Johns looked like me. Everybody
sees people who look similar to themselves. But this was
me. His black wiry hair was square cut over a forehead the
exact width of mine. There was my straight nose with a
bump below the bridge. Either side, my own cheeks and
blunt chin were shadowed in a four day's growth because it
was a time for 'designer stubble' if you had to wear a cheap
suit to work. Geraint Johns had even stolen my thin lips,
and the extra push of the brow ridges that made a frown
the easiest thing to do with the face. In an instant all my
cool was gone. The close, handwritten notes were something I might be interested in. The pathetic, sparse food
items bought became pointers to – I wasn't sure where. I
tried reading from what was on top now I'd shuffled things.
*Nights the most dangerous when* THE WEASEL *will burst gnaw
out even through bone his teeth on the bone can be a good
warning of the animal being ready to move because it can be
still in its lair for weeks waiting other times like a flash out of*
THE HOLES *and then you have to let it go let it start skarrifing –*

Skarrifing? Almost losing some of the sheets in the wind, I flicked to the passport for another look. I checked the details. Surname JOHNS, Given names GERAINT, BRITISH CITIZEN, Date of Birth 09 / FEB 71, which made him eight years older than I was. Strangest of all – at least that's what I remember thinking at the time – was Place of birth, TREBOR BAY.

Date of issue 17 JUL 93. It made this photograph old, taken at my age, in fact.

Geraint Johns' passport had been used only twice according to its stamps. In the year of issue I'd been to Morocco, apparently and the following one, to Turkey.

I had never left the country and didn't have a passport.

Just as I started a more thorough search of the other documents, my mobile found a stray signal and there was Mr Nurse Senior himself returning my message about the cleaning crew with a string of obscenities like you've never heard. Always a shock from a man of his age. 'The lease is in the name G. Johns,' he spluttered. 'Any sign?'

'No. The owner said he had a van of some sort but it's not been seen for a week.'

'And inside?'

'Looks like he just up and split. No damage, just –'

'Personal stuff to trace the little bollock?'

Further along the lane a tractor turned over. Farmer Davies having let me do the dirty work was on his way for a poke around. 'Nothing,' I said.

Solveig Heggelstad couldn't have been more interested in my father than I was. In an old Fry's Chocolate Cream carton in my mother's room over the shop – years ago – I had found my birth certificate. It was blank on the subject. As was Michelle.

'No good asking because I can't tell you. I'd stayed on late to clear up. People everywhere – all over the house and it was a massive big place. They had a swimming pool! Somebody had got the leftover bottles, that was the trouble. I'd never really drunk before then. If the others hadn't brought me home, I'd still be there now, wouldn't I?' She was describing the night she and two friends had been taken on as casuals by a catering company to do a wedding reception. The friends were both eighteen, Michelle not even that. 'It was – it was months before I realised. I was so-o innocent.' Audrey could get no more out of her, so my chances were slight. And my mother's face was innocent still, but clouded, when she told me. I felt childish irritation then and every time remembering, because who could I blame? I'd need to grow up to become angry on her behalf – how a life-changing blow had knocked her off course and she hadn't even been present when it fell.

Once you've got a name, though, that's a start. And the fact that I appeared to have a brother, eight years older. Watkins and Nurse may have written G. Johns off, but with the name and birthdate I went to Cuddy and paid him in cash for a last known address, an elkayay, as we said in the lettings business. *Bit of bother at Mum's boyfriend's campsite – keep it between us, yeah?*

There was not that much to discover but old Cuddy found it in a week.

Geraint Johns had not lived in Trebor Bay since he was

nineteen. Otherwise I might have come face to face with him in Ferry Lane, bumped into him as he stumbled out of the Puffin Inn and we could have passed, never knowing. Or had a real scene, me – him – one look. Then again, it might have been just the thing to galvanise that weasel living in his head. I felt pretty good about myself in comparison to Geraint, now I knew more about THE WEASEL. When he failed to keep busy – writing, talking, hitting his books, playing music – it woke up and started skarrifing which seemed to be something you really didn't want to happen. Where Geraint had been and what he'd been up prior to Cosy Cot was a mystery but not one that bothered me right away. You must be hard I told myself, finding this sad, lame-brain brother and being able to blank him. But Cuddy, who was a bit of weasel himself, had come up with something worth his wedge. An Alwyn Johns was still listed at 159, Old Denbigh Road, Trebor. Our father.

On the first Saturday afternoon after this, I got off early. Still in my striped shirt and tie I drove Watkins and Nurse's shabby Escort the fifteen miles to my ex-village, passing raw just completed Abel Close where Michelle lived with her new husband. She had gone with Campsite Ted, in the end. No reason not to. The route I was taking left Trebor Bay after crossing the inlet and wound back on itself behind the Conway, now in the process of yet another change of use. It was to be an adult education centre. Skips had been dropped onto the lawn where Wes and I played football. The brick gateposts, our goalposts, lay flattened and smashed. I would have needed to park to pick out Room 202 under a mass of scaffolding even if the hard, excited knot in my chest hadn't been squeezing out every other interest.

Away from the village the lane climbed up from the coast becoming barely wide enough for two cars. Soon a strip of green poked through the tarmac along its centre. Houses and then hedges coming into leaf screened you from the sea and after Hulme's Garage, and an old wired glass bus shelter there was no more Trebor Bay to speak of. But things still had a half-familiar look, the way somebody else's holiday snapshots make you think *hang on – I've been there.* I knew round that bend ahead, or the next, was a row of cottages at a crossroads, though no particular memories were associated with previous journeys. What was I expecting? I've no idea now. I do know I was concentrating not on meeting a man called Alwyn Johns, but on finding the actual place. Big ideas were attached to this, his home, the family home. Surrounded by grounds, my father's should be impressive. Edwardian and solid and rambling would have done, with a tennis court off to the side. Or smooth all-white concrete and modern. Lawns like snooker table baize and decking to have drinks on.

Those cottages came after three bends in the road, not two. They weren't on the crossroads. A boarded up pub was, with picnic tables in an overgrown beer garden and a Nurse and Watkins sign offering DEVELOPMENT OPPORTUNITY. The cottages lay just beyond it. 159 was last in the row.

The entrance is at the side on this type. I'd let a couple of the same design, estate cottages built by Lord Somebody again and sold off over the years, so I knew it well. Sets of them were scattered over the square miles of what had been his estate. Fancy tile infills and diamond leaded lights on the outside, all Olde Worlde style – inside they had low rooms, two up two down. It never crossed my mind as I stood at the front door that 159 might be unoccupied and it wasn't. In seconds a man's shape appeared through the glass then there he was – Alwyn Johns, no mistaking him. Mid-forties – no, older. The hair was thick and wiry as mine but iron grey, eyes dark – I couldn't tell if they were khaki-brown because of the heavy brows. He was my height but much heavier, clean-shaven and jowly, and wearing faded jeans and a bright red rugby shirt with the Wales logo. In one hand was an apple, just bitten into. His feet on the old Marley floor were bare and long-toed and could've been my own. Through a doorway at his back I could see a slice of a living room, a chair, a patterned carpet and the commentary about a golf match was loud enough for me to catch, *Oh-h it's a good one! Woosnam's – yes! – that's safe on the fairway. Well now!*

Just before he transferred his attention he craned back over one shoulder and resentment at being interrupted crossed his face. Then he said, 'Hello,' in a businesslike-voice and a local accent and looked at me properly. Then he blinked – a lot – looked away and put his apple down on some piece of furniture that must've been next to the door. He finished chewing what was in his mouth and swallowed, staring – just staring. From out on the golf course cheers and applause started and the commentator's *Who would've thought that was going to happen? You'd have put money on –* But Alwyn Johns didn't care now. 'Yes?' he said.

I was set up while he was floundering in the rough – at least I thought I was. Good. Here was my father. No problem over that and nothing warm and sentimental was going to be a complication. I felt absolutely *zilch* – much as expected but also a relief. I told him my name and added 'I work for Watkins and Nurse,' not to spread confusion but because this intro formed part of the scheme.

'Uh-huh. You – you're with – the estate agents.' He was like a man under water. The frown lines became deeper and pinched up rolls of skin right up to the hairline. Ugly – they made him much older.

'Yes. I see what you're thinking but it's not about the pub, I mean the development. It's something else. Could I ask – do you know a Geraint Johns? It's a private matter.'

He nodded and backed up. He moved like an oldie and grunted under his breath leaning around me to close the door when I walked in front of him.

Michelle, Vic and Audrey – we were a family that didn't go in for much photographing. Above the shop there'd been a wedding in black and white plus a tiny Michelle in a striped dress on a three-wheeler. It was a shock to be in a room with pictures of myself taken only a couple of years ago in full athletic gear. One side of the mantelpiece here I am clutching a metal cup. On the other I'm covered in mud but with a clenched fist raised. Hanging on the wall a twin me, scrubbed up, has been to college, put on a mortar board and gown, got a degree and holds a scroll now to prove it.

'Sit down.' Alwyn turned off the TV leaving us with the hiss from a gas fire that was the same vintage as every other piece of furniture in the room. 'What did you say your name was?'

I wasn't having this. 'Before we start, could you confirm your relationship to Geraint Johns please?'

'Yes.'

'I have items that might belong to him.' I offered from my case the plastic wallet from which I'd already lifted the passport and certificates. The rest of the contents I'd photocopied – even sitting across from Alwyn, here and now, I still couldn't have explained why. I was made to do it. And knowing I had done it, knowing that the passport in Geraint Johns' name and the rest, including a record of his recent life, were stashed in a suitcase under my bed gave me power. It was equivalent to introducing myself on the doorstep as a representative of Watkins and Nurse. It made me more than just me.

He took the wallet but lacked the interest to open it. I was the important thing – his eyes kept flicking up to my face and away again, checking, rechecking. I should have been touched. 'Has something happened to him? Is he dead?'

'Not that I know of. These came from a place your son was renting. He –'

'Geraint's my younger brother. There's eleven years between us. I don't have kids,' he said.

I closed down the 'office' on our kitchen worktop at four, sending the last few bookings for Erik to sort, and decided to cook. With Janikka not home for another two hours there was plenty spare to make the mustard sauce she liked for fish, or walk down to the supermarket for eggs and meat, refreshing my story as I went. Alesund is the sort of town you can get away with absent mindedness. I can never believe how careful the drivers are, how quiet the streets, empty enough for you to step out into any road any time and have a good chance of making it across. A forgiving place. Just its remoteness gives a sense of security that's more than latitude. Its heights and depths, all the difficulties of rock walls that force the town into strips, and the deep water close in for the berthing ships, they're also defences against the outside. And then to survive this far north is a never-ending festival. You can see it in the public smoking and private drinking and shooting up – the way they'll brave the cold and stalk the sun. Look at her, for instance, this one just outside my window. I know her, she comes every day about now, a tough middle-aged woman in trekking shorts and a T-shirt with cut off sleeves. She brings a tiny dog into the park so it can shit on the grass – no big deal, like all Alesundians, she's there with her bag almost before it drops – but the problem is the animal won't concentrate. It's rabid for birds, chasing the crows and magpies, jumping into the air and snapping, while the birds cackle and drive it demented. It whizzes from the nearest cherry to the proper big trees that are all knobby and deformed with pruning. The birds fly back and to and this mad gremlin goes spinning after them. It can launch itself maybe a metre off the ground, tops. The birds bank on this, gliding low for maximum annoyance. If Janikka were here she'd be laughing – every time it makes her laugh. She'd be saying, 'See! See! She's here again with crazy hound.'

*Yeah, I know.*

I walk out. On the seat in a patch of sun a young couple are being entertained by crazy hound. They have their child between them and the mother is trying to feed it chips and sliced sausage from a polystyrene bowl. All three of the family are ridiculously perfect, blond, and with a slight gold sheen to the skin you don't get anywhere else. Janikka has it. Solveig has it.

All three look up as I pass – and smile.

*Only child* – I start again in my head – *of a single mother*. Happy, though with grandparents that spoilt me. I couldn't do anything wrong, could I? Of course I was curious about my father. No mystery though. It was a one-night stand and they were both just teenagers. I was twentysomething when I tracked him down. He and my mother, they'd lost touch which was nobody's fault. He'd moved hundreds of miles away. Very nice guy! I was well-impressed with the house, a great big house – he'd been a golfer, could've been top class but was injured in – in a car accident. So he started his own business selling sports gear. Had the contacts, didn't he? *Mega* success. Yes, a wife. She made me really welcome. I wasn't a secret, she knew he had a child somewhere. She already had one herself when they married. She told me later she'd been encouraging him to find me and then one day, there I was! On the doorstep.

I know, *I know*. But to be honest, they were just nice people – and strangers. It was like – well can you remember when your parents took you see their friends? Even if they asked what you were good at in school, did you win that match, come on Janikka, how bored were you? How glad were you to get away again?

At Remi 1000 I buy gravilax and rye bread and a pizza for myself for tomorrow and try to keep my mind off the story now. More will mean worse. Don't add extras. Keep it simple. The only bit of Vic's wisdom I can remember was the shorter the rope, the fewer the knots. Think about where you are now – and that your favourite building in Alesund is coming up, with the iron balconies like arched branches and the pattern of little red fruits all across its first floor.

The mood lasted me home. When Janikka came in, it lasted us through the meal and how-was-your-day and I sat with a Hansa while she ate apple jam with her ice cream and her dimples came and went at the line I was spinning her.

'We could go visit. This summer – we go there, see where you're born in. I'm sorry your mother doesn't live now. Then we go see your father and his new wife. In London.'

'Na.'

'Yes. Be good. London.' Her nodding was an encouragement, as though she was offering me the city.

'Not for me.' Why not for me, though? 'He'll just think I'm after his money. It's been years. He'll think I'm on the make. And –'

'No.'

'– he travels a lot so he might not even be there.'

*If you hear anything, let me know, eh?* Alwyn Johns had said as I was leaving that day. *You know where to find me.* It was written across his face that I wouldn't – hear anything or return. Geraint, *the clever one*, had been inching towards the edge of the cliff for years, since the day of that degree ceremony, the final time he had given them anything to be proud of. No holding back the details, not with my face. Outpatients, hospitals, endless medications. Both parents had died since his last contact with his brother and it was likely Geraint didn't even know it. When the plastic wallet fell from his grip he'd watched the scribbled pages come to rest around his bare feet and said. 'Christ! There used to be wads of that sort of crap all over his room. Not normal stuff, you know? How there were zombies or ghosts or something everywhere – and only he noticed. Did you read any?'

I shook my head.

'Too right.'

When I brought up the necessary subject of rent outstanding, those ridges in his forehead came up again like rods under the skin. He said quickly. 'I'm on disability. A fall at work.'

Probably it was round about here I decided not to bother. What was to be gained from knowing Alwyn Johns with his ailments and his barking brother, my uncle, who could be gone already? Dead ends, both. Ten minutes and I was well desolate and could imagine instructing Pugh's the house clearers, that same old Darrell, to strip it right out before it went on the market, every last stick. *What about the photos and that trophy thing?* Darrell Pugh saying. *Na – take the lot.* Michelle was better off in ignorance and getting along with the campsite owner when we'd last spoken.

'I don't own the house,' Alwyn Johns said.

'Well I can't promise Watkins and Nurse won't try to recover the amount due.'

'They can try all they like.'

Lying to Alwyn Johns was one thing – I owed him nothing. After that first quick shock of my appearance, I'd been dropped. Geraint had sneaked back into his talk. His own son is sitting across from him and he's going *Every type of pill they've tried him on – either they do no good or the stupid little bastard wouldn't stick to 'em.* But I can't pretend I enjoyed lying to Janikka. I thanked my luck she wasn't the nit-picking Solveig sort. The subject of my father didn't outlast the ice cream and we passed the evening together as we had done so often, she describing the stream of tourists wanting the same thing – What To See In Alesund – when all they needed to do was look up. To enjoy Norway you need strong neck muscles. You find yourself on the edge of the fjord or a valley bottom – very close the mountain rears up and above what you've mistaken for a cloud is another mountain at its back and so on. Up and up till you're wondering if you'll find sky. In town every building on every street is worth the backward stretch. What To See In Alesund? Everything, Janikka should say.

'We could go to Wales, end of the summer when things cool off.' I meant the business. Where was the harm? There were half a dozen places along the coast that could pass for my birthplace, houses I'd been into and could describe in detail. See that one? It's got a hall floor of coloured tiles, like a jigsaw and there's this midget doorway into an attic –

This, here on the left, is where my grandfather was born.

I had a friend lived in that street when I was at school, Mikey Jones.

He died when he was only ten.

Measles – no! Meningitis.

Once we'd stacked the dishwasher I pulled down the blinds and got her to play Super Mario Galaxy 2 with me which she loved. We had a second Wii controller for her to collect Coins and Star bits and I had my maximum thirteen lives which is a wonderful feeling at the back of every move you make. But I couldn't lose myself there saving the princess. I kept wanting to look into Janikka's eyes, check we were OK. 'We're OK, yes?' I said, still in the Observatory.

'Ye-es.'

But I repeated it later, forgetting I'd already asked and catching twin planets in her eyes and then puzzlement. 'I say yes. We go to Wales later. Hey you are not so good tonight! The princess is – toast!' she jeered.

While she was getting undressed I let her see me watching. The bedroom was small so she did it close-up, just at the foot of the bed I was already in. This is the best bit. First the white blouse with its streak of apple jam across one breast is unbuttoned and dropped. Underneath it the bra is two pure white half-moons with her flesh tight above them. 'Leave that on. Skirt now.' The skirt has no zip, is made of Lycra. She wriggles as the narrow waist stretches across the width of her hips and then rolls it down the thighs. Tights are something I find really ugly and these have a seam coming up between her legs that wanders across her belly like an old scar. They're the colour of sticking plaster – and they stick to her like cling film as she struggles free. I feel relieved when they're gone. The white thong is minute. 'Just pick that stuff up before you take any more off. You don't want to leave it all over the floor.' She giggles, and turns around groping on the carpet for things in the shadow cast by the single lamp. Her buttock-muscles work as she prolongs the search. 'Definitely not missed anything?' I hold the quilt up and she slides under it, reaching for me and I make a big thing of breathing her in. Her smell was what first made me think it could work between us, how hers was just warm skin or, at worst, soap and peppermint, never perfumed, nothing artificial. Her deodorant is a bar of rock crystal Solveig buys for her when she can't get it here. The only detectible thing is a cream for her face that she says has marigolds in it but she won't put it on until after the shower she'll get up and have before we sleep.

She sits across me and bends to grab onto my biceps, which I started work on in jail and have kept up. 'Very gloo-omy arms,' she whispers, kneading, her hair falling over my face. 'Cheer up shoulders.'

I shut my eyes to give fantasy a chance.

Though I say it myself I'm a good finisher – thirty seconds after I close it down Janikka is a sizable heap with her back along my side and her head tucked into the pillow. The rigid wire inside a cup of her bra has got itself under one of my thighs and I'm suddenly aware of the thing but I stay static. Here comes the first very soft snore. A few more and I'm able to slide the thing out from under, slide away myself.

This is the best time, the room taken down to a sort of

silver by the lamp, nobody on foot beyond our windows, maybe just a car a minute passing down on Storledbakken. Last time I lay like this I heard what I thought was an owl and nothing else apart from Janikka's snoring, which I'm fine with. Until Janikka I hadn't experienced how someone's fault – I'm only calling it that because of what I've heard, I don't say it is – is a fault and at the same time being able to like it. It makes her more loveable and makes me want to smooth out the twisted ropes of hair pasted to her spine with sweat – all because of a fault. Where's the sense? But I carry on with this, letting my imagination tour the rest of Janikka hidden under the quilt. Her shoulders are broad as mine, though less well developed, her breasts with their plum nipples are really taut. She complains she has 'not a waist' if I compliment her which isn't true because she's long bodied so there's just a long curve in and then out again to wide hips. In preparation for moving and waking her, I visualise her thighs, hard and rounded with no hint of fat – and then the phone rings. I grab for it and sit up but already Janikka's snore has stopped and changed in midair to an Ah-hh, like a sound on the way to being a word. 'Shush,' I say and get up and walk next door but the bed creaks with her surfacing.

'*Ja?*'

Barely a pause, then a woman's voice says slowly and deliberately in accentless English. 'No one is just what you see.'

My throat nearly closes up on me. 'What?' is a croak.

'*Ingen er bare det du ser.* No one is – maybe only what you see on the outside?'

'Who's this?'

Mean, female laughter answers the question for me.

'Who is it?' Janikka calls from the bed.

'It's Solveig,' I say and Solveig says, almost in sync.

Solveig adds, 'How are you Geraint?'

In a flash the complete Solveig is there in my head with her thin, spiky body, her hair darker than Janikka's and cut close into points. There are brown scalpel blades in front of each ear, a V in the centre of a high forehead, even a claw of hair at the nape of her neck. Her skull is perfection, not a lump or bump on it, and her cheek bones are fine but very evident with hollows underneath. Only her eyes are the same as Janikka's, speckled grey though even they're sharper, colder. She'll get worry lines soon. For now she's faultless. 'Can I talk to Janikka? She asked me to –'

'Here,' I say, handing over the phone. They go at it in Norwegian, way beyond my speed. Only the giggling, I get. I walk off to find myself a beer and come back to Janikka gone, the shower running. Can't wait – 'What was that about?' I call.

She comes out in a cloud of steam, naked and shiny, the white towel like a turban, wrapping her pink face. 'We couldn't remember,' she said, stretching to adjust the headgear.

'Remember what?'

'Yes. I will say. Solveig and me we couldn't remember the writing by the statue of the – oh – you know him, *den tigger* – poor man? In Bergen – outside the building. He is sitting – he is *laying* next to the big wall at the door in Tor-galmenningen – with the no shoes? I think it is a bank. The door of a bank and he died there from being poor long ago. And they made the statue. We liked him when we were little girls. But we couldn't remember the words with him and we were too lazy – we didn't go look. Solveig went today.'

I knew the statue which should have been calming. 'Good.'

'*Ja*. Solveig is good.'

Janikka is good. Janikka saved me that third and worst time.

I blame Alwyn Johns. I was doing fine until I went to see Alwyn. Although nothing else connected with him happened because Watkins and Nurse decided to swallow the loss on account of how I made the case for Geraint Johns *being a dead 'un* – I still hold Alwyn responsible. My room in the house share was the same – better, I painted it. My job was the same and my commission was rising all the time as I got to know the angles, how to take a slice from Pughs' when I brought a clearance in, a slice from the decorator for a cosmetic job to get a shabby flat back on the market. But I wasn't the same – nor getting better. The memory of Alwyn's shuffle and his bare feet like mine and the old people's belongings all round him – not to mention words and whole sentences from Geraint's ramblings – they found their way into me. If you've ever been to a refurb – and what you have to do is be careful, you touch nothing – still you come out tasting plaster dust and, later, you'll find a smear on you somewhere.

There'd be nights I'd lie in the dark and go over the talk we should have had. Not an *Oh Dad oh Son* teleflick talk but me giving him what I thought of him about his treatment of Michelle and him breaking down, begging. I'm glad I've turned up still in my suit with the Watkins and Nurse canvas case, so he sees how well I'm doing. And in the dark it was a better suit, quality tailoring, it was the stone linen, three buttoned job Dewi Langford, the solicitor, sometimes wore to an auction at one of the big hotels.

Of an evening, I took to driving out and parking up at the crossroads in the empty pub's beer garden. Half shielded by bushes you could watch 159 Old Denbigh Road and a light might come on in the shabby front sitting room but usually only the glow from the TV told you someone was home. Alwyn Johns never came out. A van did pull up once and Alwyn opened the door to its driver, shook his head and pointed back the way it had come, watching till it was out of sight. Loser, I mouthed at him. He couldn't see.

The daffodils in the beer garden poked up through the weeds, flowered and died off to brown paper and I was still at it.

I started visiting Abel Close more. Michelle was the same quiet Welsh girl but even softer bodied and more of her, nearing forty. But you could tell Ted thought himself well in credit by the way he just stared and stared as she sat there on the suede three piece or passed the tea round. Months after I'd tracked Alwyn down, high summer by then, I dropped by and she took me to one side – Ted was outside fiddling with his barbecue – and she said, 'I've got something to tell you.'

*Alwyn Fucking Johns*, I thought. He's turned up here. Started asking questions – luckily before I could make an

idiot of myself she said, 'I wanted to tell you, first – after
Ted. I haven't even told your gran yet. I'm having a baby.'

'Yeah?' I said.

She smiled and flushed, her few freckles standing out.
I can remember trying to count them when I was little,
getting to twenty, giving up. 'I can't believe it myself. Like
a miracle. We – Ted and me – we're really pleased. It's early
days yet but we're so – oh, Ted's over the moon.' We both
looked at Ted on the other side of the patio doors, hair
thinning but a wiry old cowboy still. And active, chiselling
the burnt remnants off his grill with a wallpaper scraper,
sending them flying onto the flags. 'That's – excellent,' I
said. I meant it. Suddenly she looked the proper mother, in
her pink frilly top and a skirt that came down to brush her
calves. Ted was generous I knew and for the first time in
her life Michelle could dress as she wanted and this was it.
Pink. Frills. Strappy shoes. Like those women who got out
of MG sports cars and Volvo estates in my childhood, and
wandered into Bay Vista or The Loft. 'I'm pleased for you
Mum,' I said and she cried and hugged me.

'They say it's a little girl.'

'Hey – awesome! Be just like you,' I said which made her
cry harder.

The next time she was subdued, glad to see me as
always, but – 'Oh, I'm – I was going to call and get you to
come. I was just thinking about you now. Ted's had to go
and sort out the water – there's no pressure for the showers
or something. He won't be long. I'll get us –'

'What's up, Mum?'

Instead of answering she asked if I'd been to see Audrey

lately and relaxed when I shook my head. That was just as well, she said, because, oh Christ – she hadn't got round to telling her about the baby, just hadn't, you know, and now she was thankful because the baby – there wouldn't be a baby, no little girl. 'She's all wrong,' Michelle kept repeating. 'All wrong, see. They were very nice but everything's wrong with her, so it's no good. I'm going in tomorrow. Ted's taking me. He'll be back soon if you're staying. He's – well, he's –'

I didn't stay. There was no help I could be, nothing to say except sorry. I surprised myself with how much I meant that Sorry Mum.

Sorry for you. Sorry for the little girl, all wrong.

After this I couldn't get rid of some feeling or other and yet I didn't know what it was. Days at work went on as before – five and a half of them for Watkins and Nurse and one night a week at the College – Travel and Tourism, a breeze. No threat of sudden death from 5D smokers made it so easy now. Sunday mornings there was footie and buying a lager or three in the Old Station Hotel for Darrell Pugh – afterwards, a game of pool, keeping my nose to the ground. A local developer and his 'friend', a councillor would drop in there of a Sunday and even Dewi Langford could be tagging along in his handmade suit. I had ambition.

But I kept going back to that face staring out of a passport photo and Geraint Johns' collected works with its crackerhead theories about THE WEASEL.

*My fault because I ripped the sheet away just one time and because my eyes were loose THE WEASEL got in through them and got his eyes in front of mine so everything I see he sees*

*first I hate knowing he's seen it first hate that hate* THE WEASEL
*being able to skarrif everything*

Read enough and it starts to add up. Although poor
Geraint was a bad case of Error 404, it began looking to me
as if he'd stumbled on a major truth. While you're young
you stroll through the world without consulting the guide
book. You give it the benefit of the doubt. Drink the water,
eat the salad, forget about the shots. But as you grow, that
weasel somehow finds a way in behind your eyes and then
one day, suddenly, you are more him than you. You catch
yourself skarrifing.

When Michelle had told me she was having the baby,
'Sweet, Mum,' I'd said and meant it.

Baby crashes and burns. *Sorry.*

Then sitting outside the Old Station Hotel waiting for
Darrell who'd gone for drinks but I knew would be stalled
at the fruit machine, I see the builder that Watkins and
Nurse uses for the maintenance on our country properties
and I think if Michelle and Ted – if, say, that's it for Michelle
and Ted and it means no kids ever, then a campsite of two
acres with services in the shape of a shower and toilet block
and the newly-themed Ponderosa Bar, the whole ranch
house in fact are going, eventually, to – who?

The weasel was out that day. Darrell comes back smirk-
ing, winking, and he's got a tall, leggy Goth-lady hanging
on him, pierced lip, nose stud, black leather skirt, black
studded waistcoat, face white, lips and eyelids done in
thick black. She had a WKD Blue in both hands. She was
eighteen, maybe. 'This is Rena.'

Rena said, 'This is my friend Luce.'

It was the weasel looking at her. He saw a rabbity little thing, thin enough for a druggy or an eat and throw it up case. Hiding half her face, the hair was hacked off more than cut and it had been dyed darker than the brown sprouting from her scalp. She slid onto the bench on my side because Darrell and Rena had taken the opposite and were twining round each other like mating eels. She settled in and stared straight past them, her white stick arms on the table, her elbows sharp enough to leave dents. The black T-shirt was baggy and grey at the neckband and armpits from washing which was sad and exciting, about equal. Her jeans were the wrong blue from being really cheap. She had flipflops on bare feet and started playing with the heel of one using the other one's big toe.

'Hiya Luce.'

She turned to me and smiled with small uneven teeth on show and lips tinged with blue from her drink. Nearly pretty – her turned up nose had been caught with sun, her chin as well and it had a strawberry mark like a dash in bold, just on the bone. But what I didn't notice was all that heavy mascara and thick black lines that would be panda smudges anyway before long, were still wet, as in just put on.

Darrell had his van. We'd had two already but we have another now, and we buy Rena and Luce a second WKD each. It's obvious Darrell knows Rena. It comes out in the way his voice drops every other sentence as he says something just for her to hear, the way she holds out her hand and he puts pound coins onto it for the cigarette machine. To me she says not one word. I get her profile as she sits sideways on the bench like it's a horse, one smooth bare leg thrown where I can see it, with a shiny black ankle boot pawing the ground. She knows.

'You live near here, Luce?' I ask to annoy Rena.

Luce shook her head, looking down into her drink, giving it a swirl, then said, 'Yeah – well just – I mean I just come here.'

'OK. So – what you getting up to today, then?'

She coloured under the sunburn. '*Nothing!*'

'OK.'

Rena blew a signal in smoke in her direction which seemed to strike Luce dumb. 'Why don't you take us for a ride somewhere Darrell?' she said not taking her eyes off Luce. 'We'd like that, yeah, wouldn't we Luce? You got the company limo out the front?'

Darrell didn't flinch though she was alluding to the white van. He was on his feet, draining his glass and grabbing his keys. 'Quick splash in the pond and we're out of here.' The look he gave me said just hold the wheel. With him gone Luce fell into gnawing on the inside of her lip while Rena sat and texted, holding the phone like it was a joystick. The excitement has all seeped out of me and it wouldn't have taken much to get up and go. The builder I'd recognised, a fat shaven-headed Jimmy Main, stomped past with his fat wife on the way out. And for some reason I called, 'Another time, Jimmy.' He and his wife were arguing, I could see that just after I'd spoken, and now he turned a face like a water melon on me, stared long enough for the fat wife and Rena and Luce to register he was staring and then walked off, neck muscles bunched at the back. Luce was the one who laughed. Rena went back to her phone but Luce had to say, 'I think you just been told.' Then Darrell was there again.

To this minute, sitting in Alesund with the next batch of tourists crossing the park beyond the glass, I can't place where we went to. Darrell drove us along Ferndale and out of Llandudno Junction onto the main A55, over the river and then onto the opposite bank and we were under the walls of the castle with trippers like toy soldiers up on its battlements. Did he have a destination – or as usual with Darrell did he throw the dice and wait for what turned up? It was July, the end of a dry afternoon and most of the coastal traffic was in the other direction towards the English border, Chester, Merseyside and beyond. Still Darrell decided to swing us inland onto the lanes, McFly playing too loud to ask What? Where? He and Rena laughed and she did us a smoke, handing it back to Luce who inhaled so you thought her skinny little ribs would crack, then handed it to me. Luce and I were on the drop down bench seat Darrell had made and put in himself, having to hang onto each other, sliding around. No side windows, just a view ahead of fences and fields now – then Christmas trees where the forestry closed in. A couple of times we nearly left the road and clipped a trunk as Rena pushed her fingers down into Darrell's crotch. A mile or more of this and the van swung onto a patch of hard standing, straight across it and onto a track so uneven Luce and I were hitting out heads on the van roof.

'Fuck this,' I shouted at him.

'Don't go all girly. You gotta have faith,' he chanted.

The van gave a massive jolt and stopped. In front it was lighter than in the woods – dazzling after the gloom – but the bonnet had nudged against a wire fence. Darrell switched off and turned around with a smirk.

'You've busted the van,' I said.

'No.' He got out. Rena got out. Luce and I scrambled out of their doors.

The light was coming off the surface of a big pool, marsh and reeds all around it except from one area just beyond the fence where water came up to a gravel beach. Suddenly the sun broke through properly and the heat on the face was like a fire. It was *hot*. Clouds of midges danced and invisible things squawked in the bushes. A sign attached to the fence said PRIVATE KEEP OUT. Darrell tore it free and used it to pull the barbed top wire forward and down – it was nearly rusted through anyway – and made a stile with it for Rena to get those long legs over. He turned to look at Luce then, all businesslike as though we were about to move a settee, said to me. 'I'll get over – you grab her and pass her across.'

Luce's arm snaked round my neck and she was nothing when I picked her up, the bones of her thighs pressing on my wrist even through thick denim. The four of us over, Darrell spread his arms and said, 'Yea-hh?' Then he took a half bottle of vodka out of each jacket pocket and tossed me one. Rena's face was a mask. She touched the back of his neck with her nails, then ran them around and across his chest and walked off along the gravel to where the grass ran down to the edge again and the trees were thick and dark. It would've looked a lot sexier if she hadn't tripped on a root but they went and Luce and I watched them all the way down onto to Darrell's jacket, and then Rena rolling on top of him.

I stroked the round of Luce's head with its little ear, my insides twisting up, my mouth dry. The vodka helped that. Then she gulped some and we walked in the opposite direction till we found a hollow where a trunk had fallen away from the water and left a cup of soil and needles. 'You don't got a coat nor nothing?' Luce said looking down.

'Sit there. Hang on to the bottle. I'll just get –' I clambered back over to the van and found a piece of green tarpaulin under the seat and a high-viz jacket, bringing them to Luce like trophies. We curled up, the bottle went back and to, her knee spiky as a normal elbow against me. I stroked her hacked hair again and felt her shiver. She whispered, 'You're all right. I don't like that Darrell much nor Rena.'

'She's your mate.' I started probing down her spine, having to nerve myself to press because in my mind I could see chicken bones, Audrey with her knife on a Sunday dinnertime, jointing out she called it. The carcase looked pathetic – but then I found that one spot below the shoulder blade that makes them moan. Luce moaned. I swear her shoulder blade actually bent it was so light and thin, more plastic than bone – more doll than person. I kissed her. The vodka and weed made me sloppy. She let my tongue in and the flavour was bubblegum still from the WKD. When I gave us a breath, she mumbled, 'I only met her, just. She give her make-up –' Under the T-shirt I found a pink padded bra with nothing much beneath it. Then grey-white knickers and the hot moist flesh to flesh where the legs and body join. But after that she started to squirm.

'You OK?' I'm sure I said into the soft skin of her throat. Anyhow, she kissed me back hard enough to feel the uneven teeth through her upper lip. And it was *so bloody hot* – she was so hot everywhere I touched and my shirt was pulled off and the full sun on me – I remember thinking my back is gonna be the colour of a smacked arse tomorrow – and bright light and noises from the bushes and the bonfire crackling of the tarp underneath were all one thing. 'Luce – you're so – so –' Couldn't think of a word.

I moved on top – felt around again and was just about there when this huge sob is coming up out of her, one hand still clinging onto to me while the other has got between us and is pushing me off. She said, 'I haven't never –' and then her clenched bony thighs with the grey knickers hanging off them were enough and that was me done. It was Rena I thought about as it happened with those long legs either side the bench – like riding a horse.

I opened my eyes. Our heat combined and was too much, over us like a blanket and filling up the dint we were lying in. The piece of tarp and the jacket had become plastic clammy – and there was the soil smell and the Christmas smell off the fir cones and needles and Luce's smell, sweet and girly with a touch of soap. I eased her slide out from under me. She gave a sniff, keeping turned from me, and then tried to snuggle back but I wasn't allowing it. 'Anything left in the bottle?'

She pulled her bra into place as though there was something to cover. 'No.'

I got my belt done up and found my cigarettes. 'D'you want one?' She nodded but looking at her made her cry. Her eyes were the colour of the birthmark and that was scarlet and uber-angry now. You'd think I'd hit her. 'Don't cry.' I rubbed up and down one scrawny arm. 'You're all right. Don't. Here.'

'I never –'

'Yeah – get it, yeah. You still haven't love.' I worked my way into a better position with fewer rocks in my back and smoked, a bit wired, a bit low. Luce put her head on my shoulder pretending to doze and over the top of her black and brown mess of hair I could watch Rena, stripped to the waist but still in her leather skirt and boots riding Darrell like he was a picnic bench.

High summer meant days nearly as long as Alesund's. When the light finally started to go we lit a fire on the gravel with wood and cones and a mag out of the van. We got so thirsty with the fire and smoking – Darrell had no more drink but a steady supply of eighths of herbal – we filled the vodka bottles from the pool.

'You're meant to boil that,' Rena said. During the last hour something had happened between her and Darrell. They were like a pair of scissors now.

'Go fuck yourself, Rena,' he said handing me the bottle having gulped half of it himself, making a noise. His breath was coming out through his nostrils and that was noisy as well – everything was for show.

'What's it taste like?' Luce asked. Even she was keeping away from Rena, looking at the other two from behind me.

'Tastes just like single malt,' Darrell said. 'Here you go, Council Home.'

But I tasted it before handing it to her. 'Like drains.' Rena laughed, a first at something I'd said. But Luce drank the lot and I went with Darrell to the stones sticking up off the gravel beach where it was deep enough to get water without mud. Darrel squatted in front, his buttocks stretching that big seam up the back of his Ben Shermans till it looked like they'd split. 'What did you call her?'

'She's off the Council Home,' he said. 'The place back of Bryn Street by the station. Runaway. Rena met her hanging round The Junction. Picked her up for a stray. Lucky for you.'

Could have said a lot of things here – but I didn't. Should have said need to get back working tomorrow but so was Darrell though only for his father. Should have said need a burger come on I'll buy. Instead we smoked and drank the pool as though there was still Smirnoff in the bottles. Rena went and sat on a rock, her own island and finally took the boots off, pitching them over her shoulder, back to land. Darrell only had to go and pick one up, fill it with water and shout, 'Champagne!' then spit it straight out. 'Fuck, Rena, your feet stink!'

She wanted to go. When he was ready, he told her. So she sat on her rock half way between the fire and the sign saying PRIVATE KEEP OUT and stared straight ahead throwing pebbles in. Darrell smoked. Luce and I smoked, her lying up against me. Across the pool what I thought was one of those halogen lights off a garage forecourt some- where turned out to be the full moon, just a single big eye.

Everything was tense though. You could feel it in the quiet. Then the second time I went off for a piss, I zipped up and there was Rena behind me. 'Are the keys in the van?

'Don't be daft. Darrell's got 'em on him.'

She said, just casual, 'I'm gonna cut him next I see him.' Then straightaway she took my hand and put it on her, which was bare and shaved under the skirt and we sort of sat/lay down in the bracken. I wasn't that confident – but Rena was. 'Hey Darrell!' she shouted while she was on board. 'We'll be going after this, yeah?'

How long was I gone? Ten minutes – fifteen? I know this – once I was with Rena, I thought of Luce.

Luce was where she'd been left, in a ball now and sniffing again. But when I touched her she yelped like a dog so I guessed this time she'd fallen asleep properly and could cry in it. Darrell was a way off, standing with his back to the fire. 'Gonna split now, me. Fuckin' tedious this is,' and Rena and I followed. Luce was there somehow as well in the van, not looking at me not looking at any of us – but the one thing bothered me on the way back – I know now it should have been another problem, but honestly, the niggle in my brain was how we hadn't kicked out the fire. That was all. What if we'd started a fire? Weed and vodka were like thick fog in my head and I couldn't even make sense of the dashboard clock. 1:05. – hours gone missing. Gone missing reminded me of Luce. But I was up front, next to Darrell now. Cricking my neck trying to make her out her huddled back there as far from Rena as she could get, was too much like hard work.

But Lucille Lloyd was aged thirteen years and a half.

Darrell got four for rape – eighteen months, me, for inde-
cent assault. A place on the sex offenders register for us
both.

The worst dip of the three.

Ted said I couldn't live at the campsite on account of
the families, said it was the law. So in under a year I came
out to Audrey's old stock room. The shop was long shut,
its windows whited inside and the dead flies heaped on
the floor like spilt currants. The shelves still displayed old
copies of *Ideal Home* and *Hello!* Because Audrey's brain
had started – and then speeded up at – going bad. Sometimes the old Audrey would be in – with delights such
as, 'I always knew you'd get caught out – always told our
Michelle. She'd never have it. Stealing? Oh no he's not. But
I knew.' And these were her good days, when she wasn't
up at six, marching into my room shouting that the phone
wasn't working, no papers had been delivered and was I
going to get myself out that bed *and do something about it?*
Once she'd eaten – and only gradually – present day Audrey
returned with a few normal concerns. Had the meter been
read or was this an estimated bill because it was way too
much. Make sure to pick up that prescription – four items
not three like last the time.

Michelle said, 'I know it's not what you want but it's a
place till you get yourself – sorted. And looking after your
gran will count for a lot when you, you know – you'll see,
love.'

In the afternoons, I'd lie on the bed-settee in my back
room that had only a sky light and was smaller than a cell,

# ACKNOWLEDGMENTS

The author would like to thank the editors of the following publications where stories from this collection first appeared: 'Roof' first appeared in *Planet*, 'The Chameleon' in *The New Welsh Review*, 'A Crack' in *Mirror, Mirror* published by Honno and 'Eyeful' was a commission for *The Big Issue*.